JCH

First published in Great Britain in 2011 by Simon and Schuster UK Ltd,
a CBS company.
Simon & Schuster UK Ltd
1st Floor, 222 Gray's Inn Road, London WC1X 8HB

www.simonandschuster.co.uk
www.markgriffithsbooks.co.uk

Text copyright © Mark Griffiths 2011
Illustrations copyright © Peter Williamson 2011
Design by Jane Buckley

This book is a work of fiction. Names, characters, places and incidents
are either the product of the author's imagination or are used
fictitiously. Any resemblance to actual people living or dead,
events or locales is entirely coincidental.

A CIP catalogue record for this book is available from the British Library.

ISBN 978-0-85707-131-6

1 3 5 7 9 10 8 6 4 2

Printed and bound by
CPI Group (UK) Ltd, Croydon, CR0 4YY

MARK GRIFFITHS

illustrated by Pete Williamson

SPACE LIZARDS STOLE MY BRAIN!

TO MUM AND DAD

With thanks to Jo Beggs,
Kate Shaw, Jane Griffiths, Pete Williamson,
Aled Evans, Iqtadar Hasnain and Cai Ross.

PROLOGUE

Somewhere deep in outer space . . .

Bolts of pure energy rained down on the tiny starship, splintering and twisting its fragile hull wherever they touched it.

The huge black battle cruiser _Gharial_ lingered a moment, toying with the smaller craft, and then unleashed another furious burst of fire. Arcs of blue-hot light scythed

towards the tiny ship from *Gharial's* guns, blasting three of the smaller ship's four engines into scrap and sending molten fragments spinning off in all directions.

The last remaining engine tried to drag the little starship to safety, but a further blast from its attacker sliced it clean off the ship. The detached engine coughed out a thin wisp of vapour and expired. The little craft sat paralysed against the harsh blackness of space.

One more hit would obliterate it.

Aboard the *Gharial*, a radio spat out a burst of static.

'We are receiving a message from the stricken vessel, O Marvellous Fanged Dictator,' warbled Captain Yellowscale, bowing so low that his lizard nose scraped the shiny metal

floor of the command bridge.

From high upon his throne made of enemies' skulls, Admiral Skink, Grand Ruler of the Swerdlixian Lizard Swarm and commanding officer of the *Gharial*, surveyed his underling with huge, cold eyes. 'I suppose they want to plead for their wretched lives,' he said with a snort.

'You are indeed correct, O Wisest and Most Violent Lizard Emperor,' said Yellowscale. 'Shall I relay the message?'

'Why not?' said Admiral Skink, popping a Dysonian sparkworm – his favourite snack – into his huge jaws. 'I could do with a chuckle.' He bit down on the sparkworm, sending its delicious flammable juices oozing down his throat.

'It shall be done, O Gorgeous

and Powerful Vanquisher of the Ganthorian Battle Mammoths,' cooed Yellowscale and stabbed a button on his control panel. A thin, desperate voice echoed around the bridge.

'We have no hostile intent,' it said. 'Repeat – we are not hostile. This is a scientific vessel from the planet Squipdip. We are here merely to study the formation of comets in the Poppledock Gas Cloud. We are nice people with families and pets. We recycle. You have nothing to gain from our destruction.'

Admiral Skink roared with laughter. 'Open a communication channel to this ship,' he ordered. 'This is going to be fun.'

'Channel open, O Wondrous Reptile Monarch,' said Yellowscale.

'Now hear me, Squipdipians,' said Admiral Skink. 'Your kind really makes me sick.

Prancing about the universe collecting your weedy scientific data. Studying gas clouds? What use is that to anyone? Why aren't you out there disintegrating stuff and waging war like any self-respecting civilisation ought to be doing, eh?'

There was a pause. The radio crackled back into life. 'We do not believe in violence,' came the reply from the Squipdipian ship. 'We believe in peaceful co-existence and the gathering of knowledge. We have learned much from our research inside the gas cloud, information that may be of great benefit to your species. Let us go free and we will share it with you.'

'Pah!' spat Admiral Skink. 'I've heard some feeble bluffs in my time but that must surely be the most pathetic and transparent of all!

10

Captain Yellowscale – blast that ship into extremely small pieces. Collect the bones of the dead. I wish to make them into a coffee table to go with this throne.'

'Begging the humblest of all possible pardons, O Victorious Sultan of Pain,' said Yellowscale, picking at the stitching of his imperial war-jerkin, 'but our spies have reported odd goings-on in the Poppledock Gas Cloud of late. I venture gently to suggest that we listen to what this Squipdipian scum has to say – at least before we mash them to bits. It could be to our advantage.'

'So, just to clarify the situation,' said Admiral Skink, 'I, Admiral Skink, the Most Powerful and Deadly Warlord in All Creation, gave a direct order to destroy the Squipdipian ship and you, a worthless underling unfit to scrape

the space-barnacles off a second-hand moon bus, are questioning that order. Is that the gist of it?'

'O Mighty Iguana-Faced Doombringer,' stammered Yellowscale. 'No offence was meant by–'

'Yes or no?' said Admiral Skink.

Captain Yellowscale sighed. 'Yes,' he said and winced.

'Come here,' said Admiral Skink, motioning to the area in front of his throne with his huge clawed hand. 'Stand before me.'

'At once, O Magnificent Terror of the Skies,' said Yellowscale as he scuttled to where his master was pointing.

'Do you know what the penalty is for insubordination aboard this starship?' asked Admiral Skink.

'Alas, O Supreme Lizard Warrior,' began Yellowscale. 'I do not.'

Admiral Skink opened his mighty jaws and unleashed a gigantic torrent of fire. The very air itself frazzled and singed. Where Captain Yellowscale had stood a split second earlier there was now only a small heap of smoking ashes.

'I hope that answers your question,' said Admiral Skink and popped another Dysonian sparkworm into his mouth. They were extra-hot ones – just the way he liked them. 'Now hear me,' he bellowed at the Squipdipian ship. 'I am a warlord. What I do not conquer, I destroy. You have nothing worth conquering. That leaves me only one option.'

'Please! You do not have to do this!' said the voice from the radio.

'I'm afraid,' said Admiral Skink, 'that if I am to maintain my reputation as the most unspeakably evil tyrant ever to draw breath in this vast universe of ours, you'll find I do.'

He jabbed a button on the arm of his throne. The Squipdipian vessel exploded in a dazzling flash of light.

Admiral Skink gave a grunt of approval. That had been an agreeable afternoon's entertainment, even if it did mean he would now have to go through the tedious process of finding a replacement for Yellowscale – the fourth underling he had incinerated in as many weeks. He settled back onto his throne of skulls and daydreamed of future battle campaigns. He was enjoying himself so much that when his ship was crushed to dust moments later by the Hideous and

14

Unimaginably Vast Comet Creature of Poppledock, which had just emerged from its hiding place in the nearby gas cloud, it took him very much by surprise.

CHAPTER ONE
THE CHORES OF DOOM

'Lance Spratley - where on earth do you think you're going?'

The sound of his mother's voice stopped the eleven-year-old boy in his tracks as surely as if he had walked into a wall. Lance's narrow shoulders sagged. He had been so close to making it out through the door. 'You know where I'm going,' he said. 'Blimey. I've told you

about fifty million billion times.'

'Don't be cheeky,' said his mother, a chubby woman with tall spiky hair. From a distance she looked a little like a pine cone.

'I'm going over to Tori's to watch the meteor shower,' said Lance. 'You said I could. It's a special meeting of the Knowledge Warriors.' He reached for the handle of the kitchen door.

'Not so fast,' said his mother. 'I said you could go and see your little girlfriend when you'd done your chores and not before.'

'Ha! Lance has got a girlfriend!' cried a mocking voice. It was Sally, his pigtailed seven-year-old sister. She was sitting at the kitchen table refusing to eat her Turkey Guzzlers.

Lance slowly shut his eyes. His previous

year's form teacher, Mrs Bellflower, had taught her class how to deal with stress by picturing a relaxing image at times of anxiety. The idea was to imagine yourself away into a pleasanter place.

Lance liked to picture himself as an astronaut floating gently through space – and this is what he did now. In his mind's eye he saw the Earth far below him, its feathery clouds gliding across vast expanses of sapphire-blue ocean, all his troubles ten thousand miles away and unable to reach him.

He spent a lot of time in space when he was around his family.

'First,' he said, snapping out of his daydream, 'Tori and me are just friends, as you both well know. Nothing more. Second, I've done everything I had to do.

I finished my project on koalas for school and I've tidied up my room and taken out the rubbish.'

'Aren't we forgetting something?' said his mother. 'Today is the last Thursday of the month.'

Lance's heart sank. He had forgotten.

Mr and Mrs Spratley ran a home business buying and selling on the Internet auction site **u-flogit.com**. They bought all kinds of things – cars and motorbikes, posters of film stars, rusty kettles, fluffy toilet seat covers, garden sheds, stuffed magpies, old soldiers' medals, board games with vital pieces missing, dog collars, budgie cages and cat baskets. After purchasing these items, they immediately put them back for sale on the same website, but with a more

19

impressive-sounding description and a much higher price tag. Once they bought a broken vase and sold it for twice the price later the same day as a 'luxury, do it-yourself, self-assembly vase starter kit'.

Like most people who run businesses, Mr and Mrs Spratley were obsessed with knowing in excruciating detail exactly how much money they were raking in. Lance's job was to go through the accounts on the last Thursday of every month and prepare a graph on the family computer showing how many items had been bought and sold, and at how much profit.

Only this month, he had forgotten to do it.

'I will do it,' he said. 'When I get back. I promise. Honestly.'

'And what time are you planning on getting

back, may I ask?' said his mother.

'I don't know,' said Lance. 'Blimey. It's a meteor shower. It ends when it ends. It's the universe, Mum. No one can control it.'

Mrs Spratley sniffed. 'I don't care about the universe,' she said. 'All I want is that graph ready to show your father when he comes back from the pub.'

Mr Spratley made a habit of visiting his local, *The Hand and Racquet,* every evening between the hours of seven and eleven. He assured his wife this was because he was doing something called 'networking', which involved 'meeting new supply-chain contacts' and 'forging links with local businesses in this changeable economic climate'. He always came home singing loudly.

'Can't I do it tomorrow?' pleaded Lance.

21

'I'll get up extra early and do it before I go to school.'

'I should jolly well think not!' said his mother. 'If it's not ready by the time your father gets back, I'm the one who has to put up with his whining. Do it now, Lance. It only takes a few minutes.'

'It does not,' said Lance. 'It takes ages because you and Dad keep your accounts in such a mess. Instead of writing down every sale and purchase in a book like a normal business, you both just scribble on any old bits of paper that come to hand – envelopes, takeaway napkins, the gas bill, my school report. I bet monkeys in the jungle have a more efficient system for counting how many bananas they have.'

'I've warned you about that cheek!' said

22

Mrs Spratley, waving a stern finger at her son.

Lance looked out of the window. It was getting dark. The meteor shower would be visible soon. He heaved a sigh. 'Isn't there some compromise we can reach, Mum?' he said. 'Some other little task I can help you out with? Whatever it is, I'll do it tomorrow along with Dad's graph – I promise – if you'll just let me go now. Pleeeeeeease?' He tried to make his eyes look as big and soppy as possible.

Mrs Spratley smiled the sort of smile that must flit across the face of a hungry crocodile as it spies a wildebeest innocently sauntering down to the river for a quick drink and a paddle. 'There is a certain little task you could do, actually, Lance. Now that I think about it.'

23

Lance frowned, trying to think what task she was referring to, and then his eyebrows suddenly rocketed upwards like startled birds. 'You don't mean what I think you mean, do you?' he asked in a quavering voice.

Mrs Spratley nodded. 'It's got to be done, Lance. We've been putting it off for months. That thing's a public health hazard. I'm surprised the council haven't been round here to condemn the whole house because of it.'

'But I hate going near it. It's gross!'

'And getting grosser by the day,' said Mrs Spratley. 'Which is why it needs a thorough cleaning.'

Lance had read in a computer magazine that it was common for keyboards to acquire dirt over their lifetime. Eyelashes,

24

flakes of dead skin, globules of earwax, toast crumbs, sesame seeds – all these items had a habit of falling down between the keys and accumulating into a layer of stinky black sludge. The magazine had advised you to clean out your keyboard every few weeks to prevent this substance building up. All you had to do was turn the keyboard upside down and place it on a sheet of paper. You gave the back a few taps, lifted up the keyboard and then marvelled with disgust at all the horrible, grimy scraps of unpleasantness that dropped out.

But none of the Spratleys had ever performed this simple act of hygiene since they bought the family computer six years previously. Consequently, its keyboard was dirty. Very dirty. Things-living-in-it dirty.

Lately, Mr Spratley had taken to wearing washing-up gloves whenever he used it.

Lance grimaced. 'Okay,' he said, gritting his teeth. 'I'll do it. I'll clean out the keyboard.'

'Promise?' said Mrs Spratley.

'I promise,' said Lance. There was no escaping it this time. He would have to borrow some industrial cleaning fluid from somewhere. Or maybe a flamethrower...

'All right,' said his mother. 'If you'll do that and take Sally to the park tomorrow after school I think we have a deal.'

'What?' said Lance. 'Not that too? You're kidding me?' He was still angry with his sister for getting jam all over his microscope; she had an awful knack of casually ruining his most prized possessions.

'That's my final offer,' said Mrs Spratley.

'Oh, fine, fine. Whatever,' muttered Lance. 'That's all I'm good for, isn't it? Doing all the horrible jobs that no one else can be bothered with.' He zipped up his coat and was out of the door before his mother could attach any more conditions to letting him leave. Putting his head down, he sprinted up the alleyway as fast as he could. Behind him, he heard his sister's voice:

27

'Ha! Lance has got to take me to the park!'

Lance had another image he liked to summon up at stressful times and it popped into his head now. He gave a grim chuckle. It was an image of him dressed as a futuristic space hero called Zork Bullfree, swooping down at his house in a rocket pack and blowing his family to smithereens with a disintegrator gun.

The Braintwizzler 360 Mind Migration System™ represents the very latest in starship safety technology. By purchasing one you have proved yourself to be not just a fearsome and bloodthirsty lizard warrior, but also a safety-conscious one too! Please take a few minutes to read these easy-to-follow instructions and familiarise yourself with its operation.

INSTALLATION

Order an underling to install it for you. To speed up installation, threaten to feed him to a carnivorous ice-crab.

OPERATION

To operate the Braintwizzler 360™ press the large red button on the unit that says OPERATE on it in big letters (see fig 1.). Your underling will offer to do this for you if he has any sense.

Fig 1.

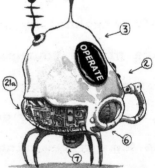

CLEANING

Who cares? That's underling business.

FREQUENTLY ASKED QUESTIONS

<u>HOW DOES IT WORK?</u>

Simple! The Braintwizzler 360™ offers practical immortality through the use of an Ultra-High-Powered Neural Scanning Network and a 90 TwiggaByte self-propelled spaceworthy memory wafer.

<u>THAT WAS SIMPLE, WAS IT?</u>

It was to us. But then we have all got Advanced Degrees in Quantum Consciousness Information Theory.

<u>I HAVEN'T. HOW ABOUT EXPLAINING IT IN TERMS A BUSY LIZARD WARRIOR CAN UNDERSTAND AND BEING SHARPISH ABOUT IF YOU DON'T MIND?</u>

Okay, okay! How about this? If your spaceship gets damaged, the machine instantly scans your mind and fixes its pattern onto a memory wafer. The memory

Fig 2.

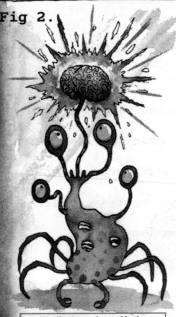

NO aliens were harmed in the
making of this image (unfortunately)

wafer (see fig 2.)
ejects into space
and crashlands on
the closest habitable
planet disguised as
a meteorite. It then
downloads your mind
into the nearest
creature capable of
supporting it.

HANG ON. SO IN THE EVENT OF AN ACCIDENT
MY MIND GETS TRANSFERRED INTO THE BODY
OF SOME INFERIOR BEING ON SOME RANDOM
ALIEN PLANET? I DON'T LIKE THE SOUND OF
THAT. I COULD END UP AS A SLUG OR SOMETHING!

Relax, it's only temporary! Just don't
forget to retrieve the memory wafer once
you've landed on the planet and activate

its homing signal so your fleet can come and pick you up. Once safely back on Swerdlix, we can grow you a copy of your original body from our genetic databanks and upload your mind back into it from our central back-up system. Hey presto! You're good as new again!

BUT WHY BOTHER STICKING MY MIND INTO SOME ALIEN CREATURE? WHY NOT JUST HAVE THE MEMORY WAFER FLY TO MY HOME PLANET? Sadly, a mind degrades if stored on a memory wafer for too long. Much better to have it housed within an organic life form. Never fear, you'll remain your usual lizard self on the inside and still enjoy baking hot temperatures, mindless thuggery and the taste of Scramthorn plants! Swapping your mind into this new body also offers the perfect disguise if your enemies come looking for you. Plus, when your mind is dumped into the body of an alien, the memory wafer absorbs the alien's own mind, allowing us to gather important data on that creature's species.

HMM. QUITE NIFTY, I SUPPOSE. WHAT HAPPENS IF SOMETHING GOES WRONG?

Nothing should go wrong. But if it does, do what we do. Blame the underlings!

CHAPTER TWO
'A MEATIER WHAT?'

'Pickles!' called the girl for the fifth time. 'Come on, Pickles! Come out and you can have these delicious dandelion leaves. Look!' The girl waggled the leaves in what she hoped was an enticing manner. Atop her head, her thick blonde curls waggled too. 'Freshly picked by my own fair hand this very evening. Exceedingly succulent. I have

to warn you, Pickles. If you're going to turn your nose up at them, I'm seriously tempted to scoff them myself. Come on now. Why not have just one, eh?'

The problem with lizards, thought Tori Walnut as she crouched by the bed and eased a probing hand underneath, is that they don't know how to compromise.

The iguana had to be in her room somewhere because Tori had only just let him out of his tank for his evening stroll. She had turned her back for the briefest of moments to retrieve the dandelion leaves from her coat pocket – and now the pesky lizard was nowhere to be seen.

'Oh, where are you, Pickles?' she called as her hand slid over the dusty carpet. 'I can't feed you if you're going to spend all

your time hiding.' But all she found under the bed was ancient toast crumbs and a fluff-covered penny.

Tori was an orphan and lived with her aunt, Hazel, a volunteer for the local branch of the RSPCA. Their house was filled with sick and injured animals that Aunt Hazel had brought home to care for. The airing cupboard was full of hedgehogs, in the living room rabbits lurked under sofa cushions, and a three-legged baby deer called Elizabeth had recently taken up residence in the downstairs loo. The whole house was filled with grunts and bleats and stray hairs and feathers and smelled very much like the underside of a farmer's boot.

None of this bothered Tori. It was what she had known all her life. But unlike her aunt

37

she could never get emotionally attached to any of the creatures that shared their home. Fluffy big-eyed mammals and birds didn't melt her heart in the way they seemed to do for everyone else. But then one day Aunt Hazel brought home something long and green that she had found abandoned in the park. The iguana had hard green scales that glittered and long thin toes that ended in sharp claws, and when Tori had first held him she got the distinct impression that he found this contact somewhat distasteful, as if reptiles were above all that cutesy mammal stuff. Tori fell in love immediately. She asked if she could look after him herself and Aunt Hazel consented. After scouring the library for books about reptile care, Tori bought her new friend a special tank

and an ultraviolet light. Pickles (as she soon named him) took pride of place in her bedroom, a lone, haughty reptile in a house filled with mammals and birds.

But he was a wilful beast.

'Fine,' said Tori, her patience worn thin. 'Suit yourself.' She left the dandelion leaves on the floor next to her school bag in case Pickles came looking for his dinner later.

The doorbell rang. Tori picked up her telescope, went downstairs (carefully avoiding two asthmatic piglets and a lame crow nestling on the fifth step down) and let Lance in.

'Blimey!' said Lance. 'I can't believe I'm actually seeing this!'

It was a crisp autumn evening. The two

39

of them were sitting on plastic chairs in Tori's garden with a faded red blanket covering their knees. A plate of sandwiches and two glasses of cola sat on the plastic table beside them. Lance was peering through the eyepiece of Tori's telescope. This was the Knowledge Warriors club (although Tori preferred the less aggressive title of the Knowledge Champions). Lance and Tori were its only members - two kids with a shared love of science, maths, computers and the occasional game of *Zork Bullfree – Slayer of Astromoops*. The Knowledge Warriors had saved the school a small fortune by suggesting that old exercise books be recycled as fuel for the school boiler. They had proven mathematically that if the school day were lengthened by just

five minutes, most pupils would actually get home earlier because they would avoid the traffic jams caused when Cottleton's other two schools let their pupils out. And using an ingenious system to track the serial numbers on chocolate bar wrappers, they had successfully caught a tuck shop thief who had been stealing hundreds of pounds worth of stock. Strangely, none of these achievements had made Lance and Tori the slightest bit popular with their classmates, none of whom it seemed could appreciate the scientific and mathematical reasoning behind them. They were all far more interested in TV talent shows, sport and playing war, and were, in fact, more than a little annoyed that they now had to spend an extra five minutes in school.

'I can't believe you've never seen a meteor before,' said Tori, reaching for another sandwich. 'I see them all the time.'

Lance's hand trembled as he adjusted the focus. He was glad the telescope was affixed to a sturdy metal tripod; he would never have been able to hold it steady himself. All over the night sky, thin streaks of brilliant white light were appearing and vanishing, flaring and fading like the striking of a million matches. 'We have what must be the world's brightest lamp post right outside our house,' he said. 'We're lucky if we can see a full moon. Not like here.' Tori's house sat atop a small hill, raising it just high enough above the dirty orange blush of the town's street lights to make it perfect for stargazing.

'What are you doing, you enormous pair

of losers?' called a voice.

The two children looked up and saw a familiar, pudgy, toad-faced boy in the alleyway behind the fence at the bottom of the garden. He was astride a bicycle, his hands thrust deep into the pockets of his coat.

'We're taking part in the World Ballroom Dancing Championships,' said Lance. 'Honestly, Rick, what does it look like we're doing?' He gestured at the telescope and then up at the night sky.

'Don't get sarky with me, Spratface,' the boy growled. 'I'll be over this fence in a second and wrap that stupid microscope around your neck.'

'*Telescope*, Rick,' said Lance wearily. 'This is a *telescope*.'

'Whatever,' said the boy. 'It's still totally

stupid.' He laughed a pudgy self-satisfied laugh.

Lance felt his blood starting to simmer. Rick Thrattle thrived on upsetting people, which was why he spent most of his school day applying chalky handprints to the backs of peoples' jumpers, stealing their sandwiches and throwing their school bags into busy roads. Even the way he rode his bicycle non-handed seemed calculated to irritate people.

Lance tried his best to look cool and relaxed, but spoiled it by going bright red. He felt his hands ball themselves into tight little fists.

Rick glared at him over the fence, as if daring him to say something else he could get angry about.

'Hi, Rick,' said Tori pleasantly. 'Why don't you come over and have a look through the telescope? You might learn something. Astronomy's a fascinating subject.'

Rick's squidgy face crinkled with contempt. 'Yeah right,' he said. 'If you think I'm going to do that you must be dafter than Spratface. See you later, losers.' He snorted again and cycled off, hands still deep in his coat pockets.

Lance sighed. He unclenched his hands.

'Thought that might get rid of him,' said Tori, winking at Lance. 'It'll take more than that nitwit to spoil the evening, eh?'

Lance nodded, saying nothing, and returned to the telescope. After a few second he suddenly let out a gasp. 'Wowee!' he cried. 'Look at that one! It's amazing!'

45

A huge meteor, brighter than all the others, was blazing across the sky high above them.

'Impressive,' said Tori. 'Even without the telescope.'

'Listen!' said Lance.

Tori listened. She heard a faint whining sound, like a distant motorbike but higher in pitch. 'It's making a noise!' she said. 'I've never heard a meteor make a noise before.'

The meteor whistled and whined like a huge firework. Then, to their astonishment, it changed course, heading back the way it had come, its long tail glowing and shimmering in its wake.

'Meteors don't normally do that, do they?' asked Lance, even though he already knew the answer.

The meteor changed course again.

46

Then again.

Then a fourth time.

'It's spiralling!' said Tori. 'Like a sycamore seed!'

The meteor was getting closer now, moving in increasingly smaller circles. Its whining noise grew louder, becoming a heavy throb that hurt their ears.

'It looks like it's going to–' but before Lance could utter another word there was a great bang that seemed to split the sky apart. A single bright finger of yellow flame shot up from the woods behind the house, followed by a thin plume of white smoke. Then all was quiet, save for the low rumble of night traffic and the faint yapping of a distant dog.

Tori gripped Lance's hand. '*Wowee!*' she cried.

47

'A meteor crashing right here in Cottleton!'

Lance didn't say anything. His mouth hung open while his brain tried to take in what had just happened. 'It's a meteorite,' he said eventually. 'You call it a meteorite when it hits the ground. Not a meteor. And when it's flying through space you call it a meteoroid.'

'I don't care what you *call* it,' said Tori, flinging the red blanket off her knees and jumping to her feet. 'Come on. We're going to *find* it!'

Tori strode over the spongy ground, her footsteps resounding in the quiet of the woods. Lance followed, casting nervous glances here and there, his heart pounding. Around them, the trees loomed like grey spectres, snagging at their clothes with

their spindly limbs. Moths and other small insects danced in the thin yellow beam from Tori's torch. The dank, mossy air invaded their nostrils.

Lance had wrapped himself in the red blanket but it still couldn't prevent a strange chill from gripping him as they paced through the darkness. They had lost sight of the column of white smoke that marked the impact site. Either the woods were now too dense for them to see it or the smoke had petered out altogether.

Lance froze. 'Did you hear that?' he said.

'What?' said Tori.

'Sounded like a voice,' said Lance, checking over his shoulder for the sixth time.

Tori listened. 'I can't hear anything,' she said after a moment.

'Well no, it's stopped now, hasn't it?' said Lance, annoyed. 'But I definitely heard something.'

'Maybe you did,' said Tori. 'Maybe someone else has come looking for the meteorite. So let's make sure we find it first and make it a victory for the Knowledge Champions.'

'Knowledge *Warriors*.'

'Whatever.'

She marched off into the woods. Lance looked over his shoulder one more time and then scampered after her.

'We'll get our pictures in the *Clarion* if we find it,' said Tori, shining the torch into a clump of bushes. *The Cottleton Clarion* was the local free newspaper. It was always full of pictures of businessmen with moustaches giving worthy organisations big cardboard

cheques for quite small amounts of money.

'It's all right for you,' said Lance. 'You get on with people. You'll be able to handle fame. I don't want everyone pointing at me and knowing who I am. I want one of those black bars covering my face like it does in pictures of criminals. I need my privacy.'

Tori gave a chuckle. 'We might get on the television news, too, you know,' she said,

grinning. 'Millions of people would see you then.'

'No they wouldn't,' said Lance. 'I'd get them to do that blurry effect thing on my face. Pixellation, they call it. I want to be pixellated.'

They both giggled and that was when a hand shot out of the bushes and grabbed Lance by the throat. A large figure wrestled him to the ground, knocking all the air from his lungs. Tori screamed. She shone the torch on the assailant.

Lance lay on his back on the ground, gurgling softly. He squinted, dazzled by the torchlight.

'All right,' said the attacker, kneeling on Lance's windpipe in a way that made his eyes bulge out like a frog's. With a free hand the man grabbed hold of Tori's wrist.

'I'm PC Sledge of the Cottleton Constabulary and I saw what you two did. Practice, was it? What are you planning to do? Blow up the Houses of Parliament? Right pair of little Guy Fawkses, aren't you?'

'What are you talking about?' said Tori. 'We haven't done anything!'

'Oh *really*?' said PC Sledge. He was a tall, heavyset man with a huge broad chest. Tori thought he looked like a wardrobe wearing a helmet. 'I saw the light from the explosion three streets away. And heard the bang. And now here you two are. Right at the scene of the crime.'

'But there hasn't been a crime,' said Tori.

'It was a meteorite,' said Lance, in a voice that was somewhere between a squeak and a moan.

'A meatier what?' said PC Sledge. 'Speak up, lad!'

'Maybe if you stopped kneeling on him he might be able to,' said Tori.

'What?' said PC Sledge. 'Oh right.' He released his pressure on Lance's neck.

Lance sat up and then promptly flopped back on to the ground, wheezing. 'It was a meteorite,' he panted. 'A piece of rock from outer space. It hit the ground not far from here. That was the light you saw. And the noise. We came here looking for it.'

'You two expect me to believe that rocks just fall out of the sky from space?' said PC Sledge, turning his large bullish face towards Tori. 'What do you take me for? A lemon?'

'It's true,' said Tori. 'They're what people sometimes call shooting stars. Although

they're not really stars, of course.'

'You don't say?' said PC Sledge. He frowned, his big face scrunching with effort as he tried to remember something. 'Now you mention it, I think I might have seen a telly programme about them meteor-doodahs once. An extremely boring programme, as I recall. I turned it off halfway through to watch a cartoon about a singing pig. That was well boring, too. Why is there never anything decent on TV these days? So, these rocks from space, then – I take it they're not valuable? Or dangerous?'

'Not really,' said Lance. 'They're just bits of rock. Quite interesting though, if you like that sort of thing.'

PC Sledge's face fell. He let go of Tori's wrist. 'Oh,' he said in a disappointed voice.

'Typical.'

'What's typical?' said Tori.

'No pizzazz,' said PC Sledge. 'None whatsoever.'

'No what?'

'Pizzazz. Excitement. Novelty. *Zing*.' He flung out his arms in exasperation. 'Cottleton's so dull! There's never anything interesting to investigate here. No kidnappings. No international art theft. Precious little diamond smuggling to speak of. Even when something falls out of the sky from the depths of space it's just some boring bit of stone.'

'We happen to find those bits of stone quite interesting,' said Tori, helping Lance to his feet. 'And if you don't mind, and as we haven't done anything wrong, we'd quite like

to get on with looking for it.'

PC Sledge stared at them. Then his face suddenly softened. 'Oh, go on, then,' he muttered. 'On your way. You don't look like bomb-wielding maniacs to me. You look like a pair of normal kids. Normal *boring* kids.'

'Thanks very much, I'm sure,' said Lance.

PC Sledge looked at his watch. 'Time for me to nip back to the station for supper, as it happens. Best be off.' He gave them a friendly nod as he turned to leave. 'It's cottage pie tonight. Crikey. Now that *really* is boring.'

Lance and Tori continued their search, venturing deeper into the woods. They stepped over several dead trees whose

trunks gleamed pale and exposed in the moonlight. The distant traffic noise had faded completely now, leaving only the faint chirruping of insects and the swish of branches in the night breeze.

Lance tapped Tori on the shoulder. 'Shine the torch on my watch,' he said. Tori pointed the beam at Lance's wrist. 'It's nearly eleven o'clock!' he said. 'Our folks will be wondering where we are. Maybe we should go back.'

'Just ten more minutes,' said Tori. 'It has to be here somewhere.'

'Face it,' said Lance. 'There's nothing. This entire expedition has been a complete waste of–' and then he vanished.

'Lance!' cried Tori, flashing the torch about wildly. 'Lance! Where are you?' Her heart somersaulted. 'Lance!' she called again, but

her only answer was the faint sound of the yapping dog. 'This had better not be a joke,' she called, 'because if it is it's not one of your best.'

This time, even the yappy dog was silent.

Tori took several deep breaths, waiting for the pounding in her chest to subside. She swept the torch beam over the ground in slow, precise movements like a searchlight, trying to cover every inch. Lying on the soft earth by her feet she found the red blanket – but no trace of Lance. She continued her sweep with the torch. Where Lance had been standing next to her, she saw with a jolt of horror, the ground gave way to blackness. She shone the torch into it. There was a hole about the size and depth of a swimming pool, but round instead of rectangular.

Trees had been flattened around its perimeter, radiating from the centre like the petals of a flower. Their trunks had been stripped bare of bark and branches. These were the dead trees they had stepped over, she now realised. Tiny wisps of white smoke rose from the hole and she saw that all the soil inside it was grey and powdery, charred into a fine ash. At the centre of the hole lay a twisted lump of black metal, steaming gently in the moonlight. The smell of sulphur was so strong it made her gag.

An icy thrill surged through her veins.

She was standing on the edge of a crater.

CHAPTER THREE
BEING LANCE SPRATLEY

Admiral Skink opened his eyes. For a moment he thought he had died and been transported to the White Rocks of Karr, which is where the souls of Swerdlixian warrior lizards go when they are slain in battle. It is a place where the sun is perpetually warm, where the Scramthorn leaves are always at their most succulent and where there is a never-ending

supply of weaker life forms to push around.

Once his eyes had focused, however, he realised he was lying on some sort of bed staring up at a ceiling covered in white tiles.

It was an odd bed in several ways. It wasn't made of leaves glued together by saliva, for instance, as the beds of most Swerdlixian warrior lizards were. Neither was it suspended ten metres in the air in the branches of a Wiffalinx tree. There was also a distinct lack of tailnipper mites. Whoever usually sleeps in this bed must find it soon fills with moulted scales, thought Admiral Skink, without a tame colony of tailnipper mites to eat them up.

He looked around. He was in a small room – a cell? – with pictures of mammals stuck to the wall. The pictures had writing on them in

a language he had never encountered before. He tried to sit up and as he did he noticed something strange about his arm. It was thin and pink. It had hair growing out of it. His other one was the same.

Something was very wrong.

Next to one of the pictures on the wall was a mirror. He scrambled out of the bed to look at his reflection.

An alien face stared back.

It was round and pink, with a brown tuft of hair sprouting from the top. A mammal face. It was like some disgusting partially shaved monkey. Hideous.

Admiral Skink sat back heavily on the bed and tried to arrange his thoughts. How had he got here? And what in the name of Kyross the Lizard God had happened to him?

A vision of an obsequious underling called Yellowscale swam before his mind. Of course. The Squipdipians. He had just destroyed their dismal little starship. But he had let his guard down. Something had attacked him, something big and powerful. It must have come from within the Poppledock Gas Cloud itself. But the ship's sensors would have picked up another vehicle. Could it have been a space-dwelling creature of some kind perhaps? He had heard legends of them. They were meant to be gigantic beings, vast as planets and all but invincible. And now he, Admiral Skink, had survived a battle with one!

Except he no longer seemed to be Admiral Skink. He now seemed to be a bald ape stuck in a tiny cell on a world he knew not where.

Another vague memory flickered before his

mind's eye. When he had boarded the *Gharial* at the start of his mission, Yellowscale had been banging on about some fantastic new safety system that had been installed. Mind Migration? Was that what it was called? He closed his eyes, straining to remember. He was never terribly interested in safety systems. He preferred the sort of systems that blew people up. He recalled flicking through an instruction leaflet for something called a *Braintwizzler*™ *360* . . .

Then it came to him. *Aha!* After the creature had destroyed his ship, his mind must have been transferred by that new safety system and then the memory biscuit – no that wasn't right. . . memory *wafer*, that was it – had crashlanded on some unknown planet, dumping his mind into the nearest

creature capable of sustaining it – which was apparently this skinny pink monkey whose eyes stared out at him from the mirror.

He uttered a lizard's curse. He had let his guard down – and paid the price. He vowed to exercise greater caution in future.

If he had a future.

He heard voices outside the room. Then footsteps. Ignoring them, he lay back on the bed and considered his next move. His first task would be to retrieve the memory wafer from the crash site to help his fleet locate him. Then what? It might be several days before his comrades arrived. What should he do in the meantime? He gave a dark chuckle. There was only one thing Admiral Skink ever did – and that was wage war!

Suddenly he shivered. This planet was *chilly*,

no place for a lizard.

A door at the far end of the room burst open. A small pink ape with long tufts of hair growing from its head bounded in.

'Ha! You'd better get ready for school, Lance, or Mum says she won't make you any breakfast!' it said and flounced out, slamming the door behind it.

Admiral Skink blinked. He had been able to understand the monkey's vocalisation – most of it, at any rate. And yet he had no prior knowledge of this planet's tongue. Maybe his mind was starting to absorb the language of his host body?

He gazed around the room. The writing on the pictures that only a few moments ago had been strings of meaningless symbols was now resolving before his eyes into

readable text. It was as if his mind was settling into its new home the way one's eyes become accustomed to a new pair of glasses. He guessed it was some part of the Mind Migration process, one that would allow the survivor to integrate himself more easily into the society in which he landed. Skink surveyed the pictures in turn, scanning the text for any scraps of information about this world. One was a chart showing the planets in a solar system. He looked at their names: Saturn, Jupiter, Mars... The third planet had white clouds and blue oceans and looked the most likely candidate for life. He read its label.

Earth, he thought. *Never heard of it.*

The door burst open again. It was another pink monkey, larger than the previous one.

'Why are you still in your pyjamas?' it demanded. 'And why haven't you done your father's graph and cleaned out the computer keyboard like you said you would? I'll tell you why. Because you stayed up far too late last night watching silly meteorites and now you've overslept. I knew you'd let us down, Lance Spratley. Just like you always do. Get your uniform on now or you'll be late. And you'd better do those jobs today or you'll be in trouble, my lad!'

Without waiting for a reply, the monkey picked up some items of clothing from a nearby chair, flung them at Admiral Skink and stormed out of the room.

The garments landed on his head. He clawed them off, his body quietly quaking with rage. In fifty years of warmongering

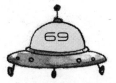

he had never been treated with such disrespect. Not even the Venom Pandas of Poddle would have shown such audacity. It took every ounce of his will to prevent himself from galloping after the monkey and extracting deadly revenge.

Patience, he told himself. (How he hated to be patient!) *Blend into Earth society. Assume the life of this monkey whose body you inhabit. And then conquer this pitiful crumb of a world!*

On a desk nearby was a photograph showing four monkeys, two large (a male and a female) and two small (male and female again). The females were the two who had just burst so rudely into the room. Admiral Skink recognised the smaller male as the creature staring back at him from the mirror. In the photograph, it was wearing the clothes that

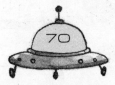

the larger female had just thrown at him – they appeared to be some kind of uniform. Admiral Skink picked up them up and started to put them on, using the photograph as a guide. Once dressed, he felt the cold less keenly.

He opened the door of the room and walked out into a passageway with more doors leading off it. A little way on, some steps led down to a lower level. One of the doors flew open and the smaller female skittered out, wearing a similar kind of uniform to him. Pushing past Admiral Skink, she pounded down the stairs, calling to him as she went, 'Ha! You missed breakfast, loser! And don't forget you promised to take me to the park tonight!'

A door clattered. A moment later, an engine

roared. There was a window at the end of the passage. Admiral Skink peered through it. A primitive vehicle of some kind was taking the two females away. He waited for the vehicle to lift off but to his amusement it trundled along the ground on wheels. If the inhabitants of this planet were so backward that they hadn't even discovered anti-gravity technology yet, how easy they would be to defeat! He let out a long, malevolent cackle.

'Why must you always do this to me?' said a whining voice.

Admiral Skink spun around. The other mammal from the photograph – the large male – was standing in a doorway staring at him, a look of discomfort on his round pink face.

'Do what, exactly?' asked Admiral Skink, surprising himself at his sudden ability to

speak the language of the mammals. His voice sounded different. It was curiously high and piping, more like some kind of rodent than the booming tones he used to hector his fellow lizards.

'Oh don't mess me about, Lance,' said the mammal in its nasal voice. 'Not having that graph means we still don't know how much money we've made and that means your mother is going to make my life a living hell. And you know how good she is at that. Can you do it tonight, please, son? For the sake of peace in the Spratley household?'

Admiral Skink considered his response. It was highly plausible that his mind had migrated into the body of some kind of slave, if his treatment by these mammals was anything to go by. It would arouse suspicion,

then, if he were seen to behave out of character. And pulverising this insolent monkey into a quivering heap with his fists – which was what he currently felt like doing – would almost certainly be perceived as unusual behaviour for a slave.

'I would be honoured to prepare this graph of which you speak,' he said, bowing low and giving the monkey what he hoped was a courteous smile.

'Yes, well let's hope so or we'll both never hear the end of it,' said the mammal. 'And I can't see that sarcastic tone going down very well with your mother, either.' It sighed a deep sigh at the terrible unfairness of existence and wandered away.

A knocking sound came from nearby. Admiral Skink guessed someone was announcing his

presence at the front door. As household slave, it would be his duty to admit visitors. He went downstairs and opened the door.

A hand yanked him outside by his collar.

'Come on, lazybones,' said the small female mammal to whom the hand belonged, her mop of blonde curls bouncing around her head as she spoke. 'We're going to be late.'

It was a chilly October morning. The low sun gave off a weak silver-yellow gleam as the two children hurried along the avenue towards the school.

'You're sure you feel well enough for school, now?' said Tori Walnut, fussing around her companion like a mother hen. 'You took a nasty tumble into that hole last night. You were really groggy afterwards. I couldn't

understand a word you were on about.'

'I am unharmed,' Admiral Skink muttered without looking at her. 'Do not concern yourself.' He rubbed his hands together to warm them.

Tori frowned. Lance wasn't himself this morning. It was as if he was working out some gargantuan plan in his head and considered the outside world an annoying intrusion. She decided to press on, hoping to draw him out of his trance.

'Fruit gum?' she asked, offering him a tube of sweets covered in silver paper.

Admiral Skink leaped backwards. He raised his hands. 'Don't shoot!' he cried, eyeing the silvery tube. 'I claim diplomatic immunity under the Treaty of Interstellar Combat Protocol.'

77

Tori rolled her eyes and put the fruit gums away. 'And you wonder why people call you a nerd,' she muttered.

A confused expression crept across Admiral Skink's face. He lowered his hands and they continued on their way.

'Wait 'til we tell Mr Taylor about the meteorite we found last night,' Tori went on. 'Blimey. He'll flip his lid.'

Admiral Skink stopped dead and snatched her wrist.

'The meteorite?' he said. 'Take me to it. Immediately!'

'Why?' said Tori, releasing herself from his grip. 'What's so important? And don't do that, Lance!' She rubbed her wrist.

Admiral Skink thought quickly, 'I need to see it again. I can't remember exactly where

78

it landed. Can you?'

'I memorised the route. We'll go after school, Mr Impatient,' said Tori. 'We said we would, remember? The meteorite should have cooled down by then. Maybe we could bring Mr Taylor? I'm sure he'd love to see it.'

'No! No one else must know about this.'

'But why?' said Tori. Then her eyes grew wide. 'You're still worried about the publicity, aren't you? Don't worry. I wasn't serious about it getting on the television news. We'll be lucky if it makes the rotten old *Clarion*, I'm sure.'

'You'll take me there? Just me?'

'Yes, of course I will,' said Tori. 'Stop stressing.' She patted his arm.

He looked at her, puzzled, as if he had never seen anyone do such a thing before. Then he

looked away and continued walking, lost in his thoughts again.

There was definitely something peculiar about Lance today, Tori thought. Perhaps he had had a run-in with his mum and dad about staying out late. He often complained that his family was driving him bonkers.

They tramped across a wide patch of grass halfway along the avenue known locally to people as 'The Lawn'. Over the years, countless pairs of feet had scored out a muddy path across it and on this frosty morning, the mud was hard as frozen chocolate. Suddenly Tori saw her companion drop to his knees.

'Shoelace?' asked Tori.

But Admiral Skink wasn't tying his shoelace. He was staring in wonder at a clump of

dandelions. 'Scramthorn plants!' he exclaimed and began pulling handfuls of dandelions out of the ground. He tore off the leaves and stuffed them into his mouth. 'Sweet, delicious Scramthorn plants! You have them on this planet! I hadn't realised how ravenous I was until I saw them!' he said with his mouth full, laughing wildly.

Two girls from their form class, Peach and Jasmine, were passing by. They looked at Admiral Skink and giggled. Jasmine snapped a picture of him on her camera phone. Tori gaped.

'Lance!' she cried! 'What on earth are you doing?'

He stared up at her, a dandelion leaf protruding from his open mouth. 'What? Is this not normal behaviour?' he said, getting up and heaving a sigh. He was unaccustomed to going this long without snarling, insulting someone or kicking something over, and it was proving quite a strain.

'It might be for a cow, but it's not something I've ever seen you do before,' said Tori. 'What's wrong with you today,

Lance? Is it your mum and dad?'

'Everything is as it should be,' he said, spitting out the leaf. 'Let's go to. . . where we're going.'

'Well then, stop fooling about and hurry up,' said Tori and marched off.

Admiral Skink watched her for a moment. Then he stuffed some more dandelion leaves into his pocket and followed.

It was almost nine o'clock when they arrived at the school. A few kids lingered outside the entrance, trying to put off for as long as possible the moment when they would have to go inside. One was standing with his back to Admiral Skink and Tori, idly kicking at an empty cola can. As they approached the gates he turned around to face them.

His face resembled a crude putty sculpture of a toad. 'Well if it isn't the Knowledge Losers!' said Rick Thrattle and guffawed.

Tori made great show of ignoring him. 'Come on, Lance.'

Admiral Skink felt her tug at his sleeve.

Rick snatched Tori's bag off her shoulder.

'Oh, no,' he sniggered, holding her bag high out of her reach. 'What have I done? How very naughty and bad of me.'

'Return the bag to her immediately,' said Admiral Skink.

'Ooh, you sound tough,' said Rick. 'Come and get it then, Spratface!' He dangled the bag above Admiral Skink's head.

'I shall ask you one more time,' said Admiral Skink. 'Will you return the bag?'

'Don't get involved, Lance,' said Tori.

'There's no sense in fighting.' She tugged at his sleeve again.

'No,' said Rick, his pudgy features squirming. 'I don't believe I will return it. What you gonna do about it, Lance? Eh? Come on.'

'It appears you leave me no option, mammal,' said Admiral Skink, squaring up to Rick. 'May your tribe forgive me for what I am about to do.'

He opened his mouth and unleashed his breath at Rick.

CHAPTER FOUR
THE WAITING ROOM OF TERROR

Lance Spratley could hear music.

The tune had a strange weary quality. It was quiet and soft and plodded along with a kind of grim determination, as if the members of the orchestra playing it had been running a marathon and had just spotted the finishing line far off in the distance. It sounded like one of those

pieces of music which is supposed to relax and soothe people who have been waiting on the telephone for ages to pay a bill or buy tickets, but which ultimately makes them want to rip their own ears off and fling them in a canal. Lance had been listening to it for only a short while and already he could feel himself becoming annoyed. He shifted uncomfortably in his seat.

It suddenly dawned on him that he couldn't see anything and this, he now realised, was because his eyes were closed. He didn't know why they were closed, only that they were and that they had been since... *Hmmm.* Now that he thought about it, he had no idea where he was, what he was doing or how long he had been there, let alone why he should be doing all this

with his eyes closed. He opened them and took stock of his situation.

He found himself in a windowless, slightly shabby room, with walls made of scuffed, grey metal. It was illuminated by the sickly yellow-white flicker of a strip light that was attached to the ceiling, which was made of the same dull, grey metal as the walls. He was sitting on one of several simple metal chairs, which were arranged in a row against one wall. In front of him was what looked like a coffee table that had a selection of torn and dog-eared magazines scattered across it.

His eyes flicked up from the coffee table to the grey-green reception desk that lay on the opposite side of the room. Behind the desk, a burly female receptionist with masses of

bright orange hair sat with her back to him, tapping away at the keys of a computer. A sign affixed to the top of the computer monitor had the words **MEMORY STATION** stencilled on it.

Lance cleared his throat. 'Excuse me. . .' he said.

'Yes?' The receptionist spun around on her chair to face him – and Lance's eyes nearly popped out of his head.

The receptionist was a lizard.

Lance rubbed his eyes and shook his head. Then he shook his eyes and rubbed his head. But none of this could alter the fact that the creature sitting behind the reception desk opposite him was, quite simply, a human-sized lizard. She had a long face, like an iguana's, that was covered in

large green scales. A pair of small greeny-yellow eyes stared out at him from under two heavily ridged brows, and a comb of bony spines hung from her neck. Completing her appearance, somewhat absurdly, was a big bush of orange hair swept up into an improbable cone shape on the top of her head.

'What is it, mammal?' she said in a hoarse rasp of voice. 'I'm very busy, you know.'

Lance scrabbled to find the use of his vocal chords. 'Wowee. . .' seemed to be about the most he could say. His jaw opened and closed in silence while his brain sang with fear and confusion and his heart raced in his chest like an overactive hamster on a wheel. 'Wowee. . .' he said again after a little while.

The lizard receptionist sighed. 'I suppose

you're wondering where you are and what's going on and so forth. Mmm? Is that it?'

Lance nodded dumbly. He opened and closed his eyes rapidly, as if this might wake him from what he hoped was just some terrible feverish dream, but it was no good. He was still here in the strange metal room with the even stranger lizard-person.

The receptionist took a leaflet from a stack standing in a little cardboard tray on her desk. She held it out for him in a massive clawed hand. 'Read this,' she said. 'It should tell you what you need to know.'

Lance got up and walked around the coffee table to the reception desk. He took the leaflet gingerly, as if it might explode at any second.

'Take a seat please, mammal,' said the

receptionist. 'You shouldn't have to wait too long.'

He scurried back to his seat. The receptionist turned away and continued with her work. The irritating music continued to fill the air.

He looked at the leaflet. On the cover were the words **Lucky You!** and an illustration of a large scaly hand pointing straight at the viewer. It looked like an advertisement for some bizarre reptilian version of the National Lottery. He opened the leaflet and read:

CONGRATULATIONS, INFERIOR LIFE FORM!

What a splendid and historic day this has turned out to be for you!

There you were, scuttling about your obscure little planet, a worthless speck of slime, and now you are playing a vital role in furthering the plans for galactic domination of the Swerdlixian Lizard Swarm! What a lucky fish/slug/quarkblat/cow/hover-squirrel/dog/carnivorous daffodil/lizard/panda/other (delete as applicable) you are!

Via the miracle of the Braintwizzler 360 Mind Migration System™, the mind of a Swerdlixian Lizard Swarm commander has been implanted into your body. We thank you sincerely for the loan of your physical form! While that's going on, your own mind has been removed and stored safely on the memory wafer that brought the Swerdlixian commander's mind to your planet. The memory wafer generates a realistic virtual environment in which to house your mind and this gives us the ideal opportunity to learn about you and your species.

Please relax. We'll try not to keep you waiting long.

Soon, the Swerdlixian commander will have recovered the memory wafer and summoned his fleet to rescue him. His mind will be transferred into a copy of his original body and your mind will, WE GUARANTEE, be transferred back into your own body. Just as well really - because your mind would degrade to nothing if left on the memory wafer for too long.

You're probably wondering what happens to you after that.

HAVE NO FEAR!

It would be terribly easy for us simply to disintegrate you or throw you into a pit or something - but we won't. As a valued ally - and dare we say it, a friend - of the Swerdlixian Lizard Swarm, having assisted one of our commanding officers and effectively saved his life, you will be transported with us back to planet Swerdlix, where you will be greeted as a hero, given a parade in your honour along Caiman Boulevard in our capital city Swerdlingham, fed on the finest Scramthorn plants money can buy and generally treated like an honoured guest for three days and nights of exceptional luxury and pleasure.

Then we'll disintegrate you.

Lance put the leaflet down on the coffee table, feeling slightly nauseous. As he did so, he noticed the titles of some of the magazines lying on it, titles like: *Warmongering Today, Amateur Torturer Monthly, The Cold-Blooded Evil Review* and *Which Laser Weapon of Mass Destruction?*

He cleared his throat again.

The receptionist swivelled around on her chair and pointed her small greeny-yellow eyes at him. 'What is it? Can't you see I'm trying to work?'

'Sorry to disturb you,' said Lance, feeling both frightened and foolish at the same time. 'But I don't really understand. The leaflet says my body is being used by an alien. Is that really true? And something about a virtual environment. . .? And then there was stuff about my mind possibly degrading and me being disintegrated that I didn't like the sound of at all.'

The receptionist sighed. 'This room you see around you,' she said in a bored monotone, 'is a computer-generated virtual environment. Your mind has been removed

Reception

and stored here while someone else uses your body.'

'So, none of this is real,' said Lance, looking around the dull grey room. 'It's all an illusion?'

'That's right,' said the receptionist and turned into a small brown fish to prove it. Lance goggled. 'You and me and everything in this room are just information inside a memory wafer, a program running on a computer to simulate reality,' said the fish

and blew a fountain of pink water from her mouth. In the blink of an eye she turned back into her previous lizard form. 'Everything you see here is created by the computer.'

'I see,' said Lance. 'I think.'

It was starting to sink in now, wild as it sounded. He knew a little about virtual reality; simplified 3-D worlds featured in many of his favourite computer games – but nothing remotely as complex and detailed as the environment in which he now found himself. The room with its flickering strip light, the metallic furniture, the torn magazines lying on the table in front of him – all of these things seemed utterly real.

A thought struck him. 'So who's using my body while I'm here?'

The receptionist pointed a long clawed

finger upwards. Lance followed it with his eyes and saw she was pointing at a large painting in a gold frame on the wall above her. It was a portrait of another member of her species, a tall, imposing lizard wearing a military uniform adorned with countless strange alien medals. He appeared to be breathing fire over a terrified underling. Odd. Lance hadn't noticed it before.

'Who's that?'

'Admiral Skink. He's our Grand Ruler. You should be honoured, mammal. It's a great privilege for him to choose your body to house his mind.'

'Honoured? The leaflet said I'd be disintegrated when he gives me my body back!'

The receptionist shrugged. 'Not my

department, I'm afraid. Can't help you.'

'And who are you, anyway?' said Lance.

'I'm merely a clerical sub-routine within the main program,' said the receptionist. 'Admiral Skink's mind was stored in this environment before yours. It left a trace of all his memories. I'm going through them and cataloguing them. It'll make a fine database of galactic warfare knowledge for future generations of lizards when it's finished.'

Lance tried to think clearly for a moment, his head buzzing with all these strange new ideas. Another thing occurred to him. 'In the leaflet it said something about using this opportunity to learn from me and my species?'

'Ah, yes. That's the main reason we

101

preserved your mind at all. Having it in here gives us the chance to learn about your weaknesses, your fears, what riches may exist on your world. It'll make conquering your planet so much easier when Admiral Skink's fleet arrives. Our Fear, Pain and Misery Specialists are really looking forward to meeting you.' She pointed to a plain black door set into the rear wall of the waiting room. Again, Lance was shocked to realise that he hadn't noticed it before.

From the other side of the black door came an inhuman cackle that made his flesh crawl with horror.

'Ah,' said the receptionist with a smile. 'Sounds like they're ready for you now.'

CHAPTER FIVE
'BEEN IN THE WARS?'

Admiral Skink lay sprawled on the ground, his nose exploding with pain. Above him, the stout figure of Rick Thrattle stood silhouetted in the sunlight.

'You're pathetic,' said Rick. 'I've had better fights with my pet goldfish. Oh, and get some mouthwash, Spratface. Your breath reeks.' He tossed Tori's bag lightly to the

ground and sauntered away, sneering.

There was no one else around now. Tori had raced inside the school to find a teacher. And once the fight was over, the other kids had trudged in to morning registration.

Admiral Skink struggled to his feet, seething. How stupid he had been! He should have realised that this weak monkey body he inhabited was incapable of breathing fire. Curse its puny bones!

'Just you wait, mammal!' he called after Rick. 'I shall have my revenge! Have no doubt.'

If Rick heard him, he made no outward sign and disappeared inside the building. Admiral Skink kicked the wall in frustration, stubbing his toe. He snarled with rage.

'Been in the wars, have we, Spratley? And not very successfully by the looks of things,'

said a voice from behind Admiral Skink.

Admiral Skink spun around. An adult mammal with a hairy face was standing at the school entrance, regarding him with a bored expression. Tori was standing next to it. 'It's all very well trying to stick up for yourself in a fight,' said the adult. 'But when you're as puny as you are, Spratley, it doesn't really make much difference. You might just as well run away. Come on, champ. Let's get you inside.'

The hairy-faced mammal took him to a large female he referred to as the 'school nurse'. The nurse gave Admiral Skink a friendly wink and dabbed some ointment on his nose, causing Admiral Skink to let out a howl of pain. 'By the Sulphuric Seas of Planet Thosk!' he yelped. 'What torture is this?'

105

The nurse laughed, 'Fan of *Doctor Who*, are you?'

Admiral Skink, who neither knew, nor cared what *Doctor Who* was, thought it best to stay silent.

'All right, you seem fine now,' said the nurse, shooing him out of her room, 'off you go.'

Tori was waiting for him outside the nurse's room. She hugged him when he came out, but he felt oddly rigid to her, as if he didn't know what a hug was for. She led him down the corridor, dragging him by the hand.

They arrived at a room filled with young mammals sitting at tables. The hairy-faced adult who had taken Admiral Skink to the nurse sat at a large desk at the front of the room, reading announcements from a sheet of paper.

'Sorry we're late, Mr Taylor,' said Tori.

'All right, you two. Sit down and be quiet,' said the adult. 'And try not to get into any more fights, eh Lance? It's clear that your skills lie in other areas.'

Tori led Admiral Skink to two spare chairs at the back of the room. The other mammals nudged each other and smirked as they took their places. Several of them were holding camera phones and watching the clip of Admiral Skink on 'The Lawn'.

'Enjoy your breakfast, Lance?' said one and the rest tittered.

'Now, folks,' said Mr Taylor, calling the class to attention. 'I have some highly exciting news. Tomorrow, we're going on a school trip.'

The class let out a collective cheer. A school trip!

'To Cottleton Museum.'

The class let out a collective groan, followed by a collective wail of despair. Eyes were rolled; sighs heaved.

'*Bor-ing,*' said a girl with frizzy red hair.

'Too right,' muttered her friend, a girl with frizzy brown hair. 'The only good thing that happened at the museum last time we went was when that stuffed gorilla fell on Lance.'

'Thank you, Peach. Thank you, Jasmine,' said Mr Taylor. 'But I think you'll find that Cottleton Museum has become a much more interesting place since it received. . .' he paused dramatically and held aloft a copy of *The Cottleton Clarion*, displaying the frontpage headline, **A VISITOR FROM OUTER SPACE!**

The class gasped. That did actually sound quite interesting.

Admiral Skink felt his heart race (or, more correctly, he felt Lance's heart race). Tori touched his arm and raised her eyebrows.

'A meteorite,' said Mr Taylor, pointing at an unidentifiable black shape in the front-page photograph. 'A rock from space crashed in Cottleton Forest. It seems it was found by a local police officer and it's now

on display in the museum. So this would seem an ideal opportunity for a visit. And a chance to prove how well behaved we can be after the unfortunate business with the gorilla.' He looked pointedly at Admiral Skink.

'So, this "visitor" from outer space is just a lump of old rock?' said Peach. 'That's not really very interesting at all, is it?'

'Sounds boring if you ask me,' said Jasmine.

'Actually that's just what the policeman said, according to the newspaper report,' said Mr Taylor. 'But boring or otherwise, we're seeing it tomorrow. Don't forget to bring a packed lunch. Now off you go to assembly.'

The young mammals leaped to their feet and made for the door.

'I can't believe that dozy policeman's getting all the glory for finding the meteorite,' said Tori. 'That's so unfair. It was us who found it. He barely even knows what one is.'

Admiral Skink stopped and held up his hand. On his face he wore a decisive look. 'I need to speak to you in private,' he said.

'What is it?' Tori looked at him curiously.

'You've been acting weird all morning.'

'Is there somewhere we can go? It's very important.' He tried to make his face look sad, the way an underling looked when he told them they would be cleaning the radiation wasps out of a reactor core. It was difficult, but he managed it.

'Something's wrong, isn't it?' said Tori. 'Come on. We'll go to the library. We can always make an excuse about having

an errand to do to explain why we're late to assembly.' She headed off down the corridor.

· Admiral Skink smiled a cold reptilian smile and hurried after her.

CHAPTER SIX
AN IGUANA'S FIRST WORDS

The library was deserted except for a couple of children who were sitting at a table poring over some textbooks and Mr Ellis the school librarian, who sat behind his desk pretending to do important work on his computer, but was actually browsing **u-flogit.com** for bargains. Tori followed Admiral Skink to a space between two

bookcases where no one could see them. They were in the Geography section, where few pupils ventured unless absolutely necessary.

'What is it?' said Tori in a low voice. 'What's up?'

Admiral Skink fixed her with a stare. 'I am not the creature you know as Lance Spratley,' he said.

Tori blinked at him.

'What are you then, Lance?' she said.

'I am not Lance,' said Admiral Skink, his voice rising. Through the shelves of the bookcase he saw that one of the children was looking around to see who had spoken. 'Please understand,' said Admiral Skink to Tori, dropping his voice to an urgent whisper, 'I may look like

the boy Lance Spratley, but in reality I am a creature from another world. My mind has taken control of your friend's body. My name is Admiral Skink, Grand Ruler of the Swerdlixian Lizard Swarm.' He left a suitably lengthy pause to let this news sink in.

Tori let out a groan.

'What are you playing at, Lance?' she hissed and shoved him backwards. He sprawled against the bookcase, which wobbled alarmingly. A thick volume entitled *Oxbow Lakes Made Fun!* toppled off, hitting Admiral Skink squarely on the head. They steadied the bookcase. 'I thought there was something seriously wrong,' she continued, shaking her head. 'Why are you behaving like such a lamebrain today?'

Admiral Skink rolled his eyes and wished

another meteorite would crashland on the planet Earth, this time one so big it would wipe out every last witless creature upon it. 'I take it, then,' he said, rubbing his head, 'that you don't believe me?'

'This is ridiculous,' said Tori. 'If you're just going to mess about I might as well go to assembly.' She turned on her heel.

'Stay where you are!' hissed Admiral Skink, blocking her way. She stopped and put her hands on her hips.

'It's the computer games, isn't it?' said Tori. 'You've played one a few too many times and now you're a bit *confused* and you think you're in it. Must be all the stress your parents put you under. I'm sure a doctor could help. Or counselling, perhaps.'

There was a rustling noise. Tori suddenly

threw down her school bag and put a hand to her mouth to muffle a scream. She stepped back from it gingerly. 'There's something moving in my bag,' she said.

'If this is some attempt at subterfuge, it will not work,' said Admiral Skink. 'I cannot be tricked.'

'There's something alive in there!' she hissed. 'I promise you. A rat or something!' She shivered.

'Open the bag,' said Admiral Skink. 'Time is wasting.'

'No way, buster,' said Tori. 'I hate rats.'

Admiral Skink sighed. He picked up Tori's bag, unzipped it and thrust his hand inside. A scrabbling sound came from within. Then a small green head popped out. Its wide mouth yawned, giving a momentary

glimpse of a fat pink tongue and two rows of tiny triangular teeth.

'Pickles!' cried Tori. 'So that's where you were hiding! You must have just woken up!' She began to laugh. She looked around again to check no one could see them.

The iguana blinked. Admiral Skink took the reptile out of the bag and cradled it in his arms, admiring its shiny green scales. 'It's a Thrall-Beast!' he said delightedly. 'I had no idea you had them on this planet.' He took a dandelion leaf from his pocket and fed it to Pickles.

'It's Pickles, my iguana,' said Tori. 'My aunt found him abandoned in the park last summer, remember?'

'Who is your master?' Admiral Skink asked Pickles. The iguana ignored him and

continued munching his leaf. 'Quiet, isn't he?' said Admiral Skink.

'It's an iguana,' replied Tori. 'What do you expect it to do? Sing madrigals?'

'On my planet,' said Admiral Skink, 'beasts such as this are used as household servants. The head of the household makes a psychic bond with the creature, ensuring its loyalty and increasing its brain capacity.'

'Very clever I'm sure, Lance,' said Tori, sounding more annoyed by the second.

'Let me see if I can bond with this Thrall-Beast!' said Admiral Skink. He placed a hand on the iguana's head and closed his eyes. He breathed deeply.

'What are you doing?' asked Tori.

Admiral Skink ignored her. He continued his deep breathing, letting the air out slowly

through his nose. 'Fellow lizard,' he said in a low voice. 'Feel my mind reaching out to yours. Feel it expanding your own mind. Feel your awareness increasing, your intelligence multiplying. No longer are you a lowly creature. You are an honoured member of my household! To whom do you owe your newfound intellect? To whom do you owe your lifelong loyalty?'

Pickles squirmed in Admiral Skink's grip, thrashing his great green tail. He opened his mouth. 'To Admiral Skink!' he croaked.

Tori's jaw fell open.

'He – the – Pickles – he –' she stammered, shaking her curls in disbelief. She steadied herself on a bookcase.

'Talked?' said Admiral Skink. 'Yes, Thrall-Beasts can talk. The psychic bond between me and Pickles allows him to use some of my own brainpower. It lets him speak and think for himself to a degree.'

'Say something else!' said Tori, staring in astonishment at the iguana.

'Something else!' croaked Pickles and let out a peculiar scratchy giggle.

Tori gaped at the lizard – and then at the eleven-year-old boy standing beside her. Her brain reeled. It looked like Lance. In some ways it was Lance, and yet somewhere inside this exterior she knew so well, she realised, was the mind of a being from

another world, looking out at the planet Earth through unfamiliar eyes. 'It's true,' she said. 'Everything you just told me. About being an alien. It's all true. It's all real. Oh wowee.' She sat down on a rubber-topped library stool, her legs shaking.

'I knew you'd come round to my way of thinking eventually,' said Admiral Skink, smugly. 'Now that you believe me, will you assist me?'

'Umm, I suppose. I've never really helped any aliens before. What do I have to do?'

'Help me steal the meteorite from the museum tomorrow.'

'Steal it?' Tori's eyes widened. 'Why?'

'It contains a homing beacon that will alert my people to my presence here. I need it to get home.'

'But why steal it? Surely the authorities here on Earth would—'

'Capture me and dissect me like some lowly laboratory worm,' interrupted Admiral Skink. 'That will not happen, I assure you. My presence here is to remain our secret.'

'Wowee,' she said softly again. 'I... I've never stolen anything before. I don't know how we'd go about it...'

'You had better help me think of something,' said Admiral Skink. 'If I don't get that memory wafer I cannot escape from this human body and the person you know as Lance Spratley will be lost forever.'

CHAPTER SEVEN
FEAR, PAIN, MISERY AND KOALAS

Lance opened the black door and stepped through into a dim and dismal chamber made of the same dull metal as the waiting room. The air smelled dank and the walls were coated with droplets of condensation. He saw a desk on which sat an enormously thick paperback book. Behind the desk sat a pair of lizards: one large and muscular,

the other small and scrawny. They grinned two wide slavering grins as he drew near.

'Have a seat, mate,' said the big lizard in a slow, scraping voice. It sounded like someone stirring an iron cauldron filled with treacle and broken glass.

'Be seated! Be seated!' piped the little lizard in a high voice. The spines on its back bristled excitedly. It motioned to a chair positioned in front of their desk.

Lance sat, his mouth dry and his knees quivering. With a hissing sound, two snakelike tendrils sprouted from the chair's armrests and wrapped themselves around his wrists, lashing him to the chair. He struggled uselessly. The black door swung shut behind him with a boom that echoed away into a bleak foreboding silence.

'We are your personal Fear, Pain and Misery Specialists,' said the big lizard. 'I'm Sludgeclaw and this is my assistant Whiptail.'

'Whiptail!' repeated the smaller lizard and giggled dementedly.

'Hello,' squeaked Lance. He tried to smile but the muscles in his face were paralysed with fear and would not co-operate.

'Our job,' continued Sludgeclaw, 'is to gather information to help the Swerdlixian Lizard Swarm conquer your useless little planet. To do that we need to know all about you. What your weaknesses are. How much pain you can stand. What makes you unhappy. How, in short, we can defeat you and your species in battle.'

'In battle!' said Whiptail and giggled, his spines waving.

Lance gulped. His heart throbbed coldly.

Sludgeclaw gave him a friendly wink. 'Before we start,' he said, 'I'd just like to say that any sufferin' we inflict on you today is on a purely professional basis. Our primary purpose is simply to extract information. Whiptail and I are 'ighly trained specialists and it is not part of our job to *enjoy* causin' pain in inferior life forms.'

'But we do!' said Whiptail and giggled dementedly again.

'Oh, yes,' agreed Sludgeclaw with a chuckle. 'We enjoy it very much. As it 'appens, we get a massive kick out of causin' pain in inferior life forms.'

Fear took root in Lance's stomach and began to bloom like some terrible cold flower. His breathing became shallow.

Sludgeclaw leaned over the desk until his huge scaly snout was almost touching Lance's nose. Lance could smell the lizard's hot, putrid breath.

'In this room,' whispered Sludgeclaw, 'we will bring your most 'ideous nightmares to life. Whatever most disturbs or terrifies you – we will find it and subject you to it. Whippy and I have an encyclopaedia here that tells us all about every species in the universe. From that we can work out what your greatest fear will be. . .'

'Encyclopaedia!' cried Whiptail and held up the enormous paperback book for Lance to see. Its cover read: **A Brief Survey of Every Species in the Known Universe by Dr J.R. Basilisk.**

'For instance. . .' said Sludgeclaw, taking

the book and opening it at random. He slapped a claw against the first entry on the page. 'See this? The Yammeldranian Gas Spider. If you were a Yammeldranian Gas Spider, the thing you would fear the most is. . .' He scanned the entry hurriedly. 'Aha! It says here that the Yammeldranian Gas Spider is the principal food of the Yammeldranian Lava Kestrel. Whippy, would you do the honours?'

'At once, Sludgeclaw!' piped Whiptail and suddenly the little lizard transformed himself into an enormous bird of prey with dark crimson feathers and a huge curved beak. The bird spread its great wings and emitted an ear-piercing shriek.

Lance gasped, struggling against the tendrils that bound him to the chair.

'Now,' said Sludgeclaw, 'if you were a Yammeldranian Gas Spider, the sight of this here Yammeldranian Lava Kestrel would give you the screamin' heebie-jeebies. So it's a pretty safe bet that you would now be tellin' us whatever we needed to know – what riches exist on your planet, how well defended it is. Anything, in short, that would help us to conquer your world. Thanks, Whippy.'

The bird of prey suddenly melted back into Whiptail's usual lizard form.

'That's the beauty of these virtual worlds, innit?' Sludgeclaw said, looking at Whiptail and smiling. 'The computer can create anythin' we imagine. Any 'orror of the universe, any foul creature you can think of. It makes a torturer's job so much easier.'

'So much easier!' hooted Whiptail and giggled.

'The computer lets you create absolutely *anything*?' said Lance, his sense of scientific wonder momentarily edging out his fear. 'Would it let you create a square circle?'

'A square circle?' said Sludgeclaw uncertainly. 'Dunno. Whippy – give it a go, would you?'

'Okey-doke,' said Whiptail and turned into a bright glowing square of light. The square hung motionless in the air for a second and then seemed to melt, transforming itself into a circle. After a pause the circle emitted a confused grunt and turned back into a square. For a few seconds the shape oscillated between square and circle with increasing franticness until it vanished

completely and was replaced by the word **ERROR** in a stern typeface.

'Seems not,' said Sludgeclaw as the floating word abruptly turned itself back into Whiptail. 'Must be a logical impossibility. The computer can't handle them. Interestin' stuff. So, young creature. Let's get down to business. What are you?'

Lance frowned. 'Excuse me?'

'You heard me,' said Sludgeclaw. 'What sort of creature are you? We need to look you up in the book so we can work out what terrifies you most.'

'I have to tell you that? You mean you don't already know?'

'Yes you have to tell us,' said Sludgeclaw rolling his eyes at Whiptail, 'and would you mind gettin' a move on because we

133

haven't got all day. I can see you're some kind of mammal but I can never tell one species from another. All you furry beasts look the same to us lizards. So what are you then? Bingerscrawp? Sky Walrus? Striped Plinkplonk? Carnivorous Daffodil? Energy Vole?

Lance thought for a moment and then said, 'I'm a koala.'

'Koala, eh?' said Sludgeclaw with an evil grin. 'Good. Right then. Let's see. Koala. . . koala. . .' He thumbed through the enormous book. 'Ah. Here we go. *Koala – small furry mammal.*' He looked up at Lance. 'Yep, that's him. *Native to Earth's southern continent* blah blah blah. Doesn't do much. *Vulnerable to extinction owing to specialised diet consisting entirely of eucalyptus leaves.*

Aha! Your species depends on eucalyptus leaves, eh? You'd be totally lost without 'em, wouldn't you? Totally!'

'I would,' said Lance. 'It's true.'

Sludgeclaw cackled. 'Right then, Whippy. I think it's time to put the frighteners on our young koala friend here. Turn into. . . *no eucalyptus leaves!*'

'Righto!' said Whiptail and with a sudden *pop!* he vanished from sight.

Sludgeclaw leered at Lance. 'How d'you like that then, you filthy little koala? Not a single eucalyptus leaf in sight!'

Lance shrugged. 'I feel okay.'

'Ha! No point tryin' to put a brave face on it. You'll be sobbin' for mercy soon!' said Sludgeclaw. He swept a clawed hand through the air. 'Behold the total

135

absence of eucalyptus leaves in this room! Not a single one to be had anywhere! Doesn't that just freeze your blood with terror, eh? Okay, koala. Tell us where your planet keeps its gold reserves!'

Lance shook his head. 'No.'

'Pah,' spat Sludgeclaw. 'Just you wait until the full eucalyptuslessness of this situation 'its 'ome to you! It'll break your spirit like a Wiffalinx twig in a hurricane!'

'Whatever,' said Lance and smiled pleasantly.

Sludgeclaw roared in frustration and thumped the table. 'Whippy!' he called. 'Whippy!'

Whiptail popped back into existence. 'Is the koala talking yet?' he piped. 'I tried

to be as much like no eucalyptus leaves as possible.'

'No he ain't,' said Sludgeclaw. 'He seems to be made of extremely stern stuff, this one.'

'Oh, dear,' said Whiptail. 'That's not good. Maybe I should turn into minus one hundred eucalyptus leaves? Would that work better?'

'Dunno. Might be worth a–'

With a sudden flash of brilliant white light, a steel cage appeared around Sludgeclaw and Whiptail.

Lance let out a delighted guffaw. 'Haha! It works!'

The two lizards stared at him with two looks of utter confusion.

'What's goin' on?' said Sludgeclaw, rattling the cage's bars. 'What are you doing to us, koala?'

'If the computer can turn your thoughts into reality,' said Lance, 'I thought there was a chance it might work with mine too. And it does! That's quite a serious problem with your computer system, actually. It's what people call a bug. You'll probably want to get that fixed for the next version.'

He grinned at the two lizards. Then he stared at the two snakelike tendrils binding his wrists to the armrests of the chair and they vanished. He stood up.

'This is most irregular!' bellowed Sludgeclaw.

'Let us out!' squeaked Whiptail.

'Just imagine we're outside the cage, Whippy,' said Sludgeclaw. 'The computer will make it real. That'll work.'

The two lizards frowned and imagined with all their might. All that happened was that

138

the word **ERROR** appeared in the air above the cage.

'What's that?' said Sludgeclaw. 'What's going on? Why are we still in the cage?'

'The thing is,' said Lance, 'I imagined an inescapable cage. So it's impossible for you two to ever get out without causing a logical contradiction. And as you know the computer won't allow that.'

'Hey, not fair!' warbled Whiptail.

'You devious little mammal!' hissed Sludgeclaw. 'Are all koalas this cunning?'

'Most of them,' said Lance with a wry smile.

CHAPTER EIGHT
THE WALL BARS OF DESPAIR

'You, Spratley, are the biggest bozo I have ever seen in my entire life.'

Mr Taylor shook his head sadly. The other boys were pointing and sniggering and high-fiving one another with glee. Rick Thrattle was laughing so hard he had had to lie down on the floor of the gym. His big belly wobbled as wave after wave of giggles coursed through him.

Admiral Skink glowered and tried once again to pull his head out. The hard wooden struts pressed painfully against his ears, but still he could not free himself. He sighed, his neck, back and knees all aching, and tried again.

'Don't do anything, Lance,' said Mr Taylor. 'You'll only hurt yourself.' He nodded at one of the other boys. 'You, Oliver Lill. Go to the school canteen and ask them to give you some butter. Or margarine if they don't have any. Off you go.'

'Yes, sir,' said the boy and sped off in the direction of the school canteen, smirking.

Admiral Skink could feel his face glowing as red and hot as the supergiant star around which his home planet revolved. Blushing was a new experience for him and one he

had decided he could just as well live without. Trust these stupid mammals to have evolved so open a method of displaying their own embarrassment and humiliation. When a Swerdlixian lizard got embarrassed his face didn't change colour so everyone could point and laugh at him, he blew spaceships up or incinerated his underlings until he jolly well felt better.

After convincing the female ape, Tori Walnut, of his true identity during their meeting in the library, the pair had hatched a scheme to reclaim the memory wafer from Cottleton Museum on the class trip tomorrow. All Admiral Skink had to do in the meantime was lie low and continue the pretence that he was an ordinary Earth schoolboy. He had tried not to meet

Mr Taylor's eye during the lessons that followed and he and Tori kept away from the other children during break and lunchtime, loitering at the edge of the playground and observing their games from afar. Everything had gone well – until now.

A prickling sensation started to creep across his face and neck, turning them scarlet. He feared his face might actually start to light up like an exploding supernova. His blood seethed in his veins at the sheer maddening unfairness of it.

Here he was, Admiral Skink, the Most Powerful and Deadly Warlord in All Creation, Vanquisher of the Ganthorian Battle Mammoths, Tamer of the Iggleflimpian Razor Termites, Supreme Scaly Prince of the Eleven Reptilian Star Systems, squatting on his

143

knees in a school gym with his head stuck between two wall bars.

The final lesson of the day had turned out to be something called 'PE'. The children were split into groups of male and female and filed off into two rooms. Admiral Skink watched as the other boys in his class changed into T-shirts, shorts and training shoes. He looked in Lance's bag, hoping to find a similar outfit, but all he found within was an empty chocolate bar wrapper and the sleeping form of Pickles the iguana.

'What's the matter, Spratley?' called Mr Taylor. 'Forgotten your kit?'

Admiral Skink nodded.

Mr Taylor snorted. 'Scared of a bit of exercise if I know you, Spratley. Well, never fear. You can use the dreaded spares.'

144

He opened a locker and tossed a large grey T-shirt and a pair of shorts at him. 'They might smell a bit musty but they'll be fine. And don't worry about trainers. You can do it in your bare feet.'

The gym was large and draughty. The icy coldness of the wooden floor under his feet made his mind recoil in shock. The boys took turns vaulting over a wooden box and landing on a bright blue crash mat. When Admiral Skink's turn came he miscalculated his speed, forgetting that his present human form had no tail, and overshot. He missed the crash mat and staggered uncontrollably along the floor of the gym until he collided with the wall bars, wedging his head stuck.

The sound of the other children's laughter came like a hail of bullets.

145

'Curse this stupid mammalian body and its stupid, stupid, stupid external ears!' he hissed to himself. Lance Spratley's body was skinny and fragile in comparison to his own, barely a tenth as strong. And it had, as he now realised all too painfully, a pair of large pink ears protruding from either side of its head. Lizards' ears were tucked away inside their skulls and never, to his knowledge, snagged on gym equipment.

Oliver Lill arrived holding a small tub of margarine. Mr Taylor slathered some onto Admiral Skink's head and neck.

'I'll say one thing for you, Lance,' he said as he began gently to ease Admiral Skink's head from between the wooden bars. 'You've turned physical incompetence into an art form.'

146

He gave a sudden tug and Admiral Skink's head shot out from between the bars like a cake of soap from a wet hand. Admiral Skink lurched backwards, knees bent absurdly, crashing into the wooden vaulting box and then collapsing onto his bottom.

The children howled with laughter.

As the gooey margarine dripped down his face, Admiral Skink felt himself blush so hotly that he half expected the margarine to start spitting and sizzling like the contents of a Dysonian Sparkhog barbecue.

A fist banged on the door. From within the house came the sound of eager running feet.

'I'll get it!' yelled Sally Spratley as she bounded towards the door. She flung it open. 'Ha!' she called out to whoever was listening,

'Lance forgot his key again!' She ran off, giggling.

Admiral Skink stepped inside cautiously. He looked around. All was quiet. Good. He would hide out in Lance's bedroom and hope the other monkeys would ignore him. But as he placed his foot on the first stair, a door opened and a heavy hand with rose-coloured fingernails grasped his shoulder.

'So,' said Mrs Spratley. 'Thought you could slip away without being noticed, eh? You still haven't done the graph, have you? Or cleaned the keyboard.' She tutted fiercely. Had tutting been an Olympic event, Mrs Spratley would have been seen as Britain's best hope for gold.

Admiral Skink shrugged.

'Don't come that attitude with me, young

148

man,' said Mrs Spratley, her eyes blazing. With a firm hand she eased Admiral Skink down from the stair and pointed him at the door leading to the utility room, which was also the unofficial office for Mr and Mrs Spratley's 'business' and home to the family's computer. 'Go in there and do the graph. NOW. All the receipts are there on the desk. Don't even think you're getting any tea until it's ready. And don't forget you're taking Sally and her friend to the park afterwards.'

Admiral Skink slumped into the chair in front of the computer. He pressed the start button and the machine whirred into life. Then he unzipped his school bag. Pickles the iguana poked his head through.

149

His fat pink tongue slid out, tasting the air.

'Something smells rotten, My Lord,' croaked the iguana in his scratchy voice.

'It seems to be the keyboard device of this primitive computer,' said Admiral Skink. 'Do not let it trouble you.'

'My only concern is to serve you, O Excellent Cold-Blooded Despot. To prevent your magnificent fingers being exposed to this revolting object, it would be my honour to press the keys for you.'

'Thank you, Pickles,' said Admiral Skink. 'It has been a long time since I last had to perform such a weedy task. Using computers! Pah. What am I? A warrior or an IT consultant?'

The iguana jumped onto the desk. It scampered nimbly over the computer

keyboard, guided by the instructions that Admiral Skink beamed into its mind. There was a flurry of clicks as its clawed feet prodded the keys. Text and images flared across the screen. A quick search of the hard disk revealed several graphs of the type Lance's mother and father were so keen on.

Admiral Skink leafed through the pile of paperwork that sat on the desk next to the PC. It consisted of old envelopes, takeaway menus and other scraps of paper. Figures had been scrawled on each of them in biro.

Even using this painfully slow and cumbersome Earth computer, creating the graph would be child's play. Pickles tapped the keys rapidly and nudged the mouse

with his nose. Shapes bloomed and ebbed on the monitor screen. A few seconds later the printer hummed and clicked. It began to print out a graph.

Admiral Skink scrolled through a list of recently created documents. It became clear that Lance's parents used the computer to buy and sell items over a network called the 'World Wide Web'. According to the flashing banner of red and yellow text on the screen, he could buy 'anything on Earth' at something called **u-flogit.com** using an account belonging to Mr and Mrs Spratley. He studied the text, clicking the mouse to bring up more pages. It was true. He *could* buy anything – and judging by the deplorable state in which Mr and Mrs Spratley kept their

accounts, he could use their login and bank account  and they would never even realise. He searched through the contents of the site and clicked the **Buy Now!** button several times.

The door burst open and the tiny female mammal strode into the room.

'Park time! Ha!'

Poppy Bossall wasn't going high enough. She had spent a significant proportion of her few short years sitting in this swing in the park and she could tell when the person pushing her was slacking off. And Sally Spratley's brother was *definitely* slacking off. She slurped the last drops of blackcurrant juice from her carton.

'Make him push harder! Tell him!' she yelled to Sally, who was swinging back and forth beside her, her head tilted back and her pigtails trailing in her wake.

'Ha! You heard her, Lance! Push harder!' shouted Sally.

Poppy grimaced. 'He's not doing it!' she moaned. 'Make him push harder!'

'Ha! Push harder, you big smelly fool!' shouted Sally.

'Yeah!' said Poppy. 'Push harder, you big smelly fat useless weak pea-brain!'

Admiral Skink grimaced and pushed harder. A crow landed on a nearby fence, a fat worm hanging from its black beak. He stared at it, distracted for a second.

Poppy Bossall's swing swung backwards towards him.

THUNK!

The swing struck him squarely on the chin, stunning him and sending him sprawling backwards onto the grass.

Poppy looked back over her shoulder. 'Get up and carry on pushing!' she yelled and threw her empty juice carton at him. It bounced off his head and hit the ground with a hollow clatter. Sally did the same with her carton.

Admiral Skink got to his feet groggily and resumed pushing. He wiped a trickle of blackcurrant juice off his cheek, his face glowing red and hot, but said nothing. *Low profile,* he reminded himself. *Bide your time.* The two girls erupted into screeching giggles and whoops, leaning back in their swings as far as they dared and kicking

their legs into the air. But then they found themselves slowing to an abrupt halt.

'Hey!' called Poppy.

'Oi! Don't stop pushing!' called Sally.

Poppy craned her neck around to look at Admiral Skink. He kept rubbing his ears.

'What's up with him now?'

'Ha! He got his head stuck in the wall bars at school!' said Sally. 'What an idiot.'

'Haha! Good!' said Poppy.

The two girls jumped off the swings and pelted towards the red and blue painted roundabout at the centre of the play area. They clambered aboard.

'Ha! Come on, Lance! Get pushing!' cried Sally. 'Or we'll tell everyone about what a clumsy blushing banana you are!'

Admiral Skink grunted and pushed the

roundabout with furious force, grimacing and straining every muscle. The roundabout whizzed around as fast as a Catherine wheel.

Poppy's stomach began to churn. 'I feel sick! Stop it!' she yelled.

'Me too!' whined Sally. 'Stop it, Lance! Stop it! Stop it! My tummy's all funny!'

Admiral Skink smirked. 'What a terrible, terrible pity,' he said. He pushed harder, then harder still. The two little girls were now clinging to the roundabout for their lives, too afraid to even scream.

'Hi.'

Admiral Skink spun around to find Tori looking at him. She was clutching a handful of dandelion leaves.

The roundabout began to slow. Poppy and Sally stopped whining. After a short time, it juddered to a halt. The two girls climbed off unsteadily, their heads woozy. They started to run towards Admiral Skink to tell him off some more but found they could only stagger in tight little spirals. They clutched one another for support, their legs wobbling.

'That wasn't nice,' said Sally. 'I'm telling Mum.'

'What a horrid boy,' said Poppy.

'Having fun?' said Tori.

'Who's that?' Poppy asked Sally.

'Ha! My brother's girlfriend!' said Sally, looking up. 'He has a *girlfriend*!'

'Really?' said Poppy. 'Haha!' She stuck her two forefingers in her mouth and emitted a screeching wolf-whistle. 'My dad showed me how to do that,' she explained. 'It's what you do when someone has a girlfriend.'

'Ha! Cool!' said Sally. She stuck two fingers in her mouth and tried to copy Poppy's whistle but all she could do was blow spit all over her hands. After a few attempts, she gave up and just said *'Whit-whoo!'* in a high-pitched voice.

Tori tugged Admiral Skink by the sleeve, leading him out of earshot of the two young girls.

'My respect for your Lance Spratley mammal increases with every tortuous minute I spend in his skin,' said Admiral Skink. 'He must have the self-control of a Sagflonian

159

Fire Puma not to go crazy with all the indignities he endures on a daily basis.'

'Very possibly,' said Tori. 'But never mind that now. Look, I brought you some supper.'

'Thank you, human!' He pushed the shiny green leaves into his mouth. 'Tomorrow cannot come soon enough. How I yearn to be free of this disgusting mammal appearance.'

'Thanks a bunch, I'm sure,' said Tori. 'Don't worry. You'll get your memory wafer gizmo tomorrow and I'll get my friend Lance back.'

'It shall be done,' he said. 'And if the Earth authorities try to stop me, they will feel the wrath of a Swerdlixian warrior lizard!'

'Oh really?' said Tori with a grin. 'Looks like you're having a hard enough time coping with two little girls.' She giggled and walked over to the swings where Sally and Poppy

were demanding more pushes.

Admiral Skink opened his school bag and tickled the chin of the iguana curled inside. 'Do you like human beings, Pickles?' he asked. The little lizard considered. 'Not as a general rule, My Lord,' he said. 'They captured me as an infant, brought me to this cold land, and then abandoned me when I grew too large for my tank.'

'Then rejoice, young Thrall-Beast,' said Admiral Skink. 'For human beings are very soon about to become exactly like the Five-Nosed Pentaxian Slime Tick.'

'Forgive me,' said Pickles, 'but I am unaware of the species. In what way will human beings resemble them?'

Admiral Skink winked. 'Why, by being utterly extinct, of course.'

161

CHAPTER NINE

A SEVERELY UNINTERESTING MUSEUM

The next morning Admiral Skink rose early and collected the items he ordered on the **u-flogit** website from the postman while the Spratley family were still asleep. He took them to his room and spent a couple of hours assembling and testing them. Pickles the iguana helped, ripping open the thick padded envelopes with his

long claws and holding screws in his tiny triangular teeth.

Before long, the construction project was finished. In his hands – hands, of course, borrowed from Lance Spratley – Admiral Skink held a small rectangular device resembling a television remote control.

'An elegant feat of engineering, My Scaly Liege,' croaked Pickles.

'Thank you, little Thrall-Beast. I would not normally lower myself to such technical drudgery but I have to admit this has almost been fun.'

'Might I ask what it is, O Marvellous Fanged Dictator?'

'Indeed. This, Pickles, is an Atomic Reconfiguration Generator Harpoon, "ARGH" for short.'

'A most impressive-sounding device. What is its purpose, O Lord?'

'It is an instrument of death and destruction, of course! What did you expect me to make? A tickling stick?'

'My sincere apologies, O Wisest and Most Violent Lizard Emperor, I meant no offence. How does it work?'

'In short, it blows stuff up, Pickles. However, its effect on living matter is subtle. You see, it scrambles the genetic information of organisms, turning every living thing its beam touches into a quivering heap of blue jelly. Ha! It is a weapon fit for a warrior lord.'

'With a device such as this you shall soon conquer the whole planet!'

'Undoubtedly. However, its power is limited.

Due to the pathetically small amounts of nuclear materials I was able to secure through the Earth postal system, the device has energy enough for only three or four blasts. You will appreciate then, Pickles, that I must choose my targets with care. Indiscriminate disintegration of this planet's inhabitants is not an option, sadly – at least, of course, until my rescue ship arrives. Instead, the ARGH is simply a tool to help me obtain the memory wafer and nothing more. Once the wafer is in my possession and I am reunited with the Swerdlixian Lizard Swarm, a fleet of mighty battle cruisers will descend upon this speck of a world and the entire population of planet Earth will beg for mercy. Naturally, I shall not give any.'

The Cottleton Museum was housed in a building of grey sandstone that had become soot-smeared by years of traffic fumes. It stood in the High Street, wedged between a baker's and a chemist. It had once been a shoe shop but the only characteristic it retained of its former use was that children generally despised being taken to it. Whereas most museums strove to bring the past to life, Cottleton Museum seemed to make it even deader and more remote than it already was. Inside, beautiful Stone Age axes were placed in display cases so high that no child could see them. A treasure trove of fiendish Viking swords lay unviewed in a chest of wooden drawers too stiff to open. And, in one poorly lit corner of the entrance lobby, a dusty triceratops skull with a broken horn

– the museum's sole dinosaur exhibit – languished atop a pile of uncatalogued rocks, its hollow eye sockets staring out blindly at the uninterested hordes that tramped past it every day.

Mr Taylor's class arrived in the entrance lobby, stamping their feet on the wooden floor and rubbing their hands together to warm themselves after their walk.

Admiral Skink groaned. Tori saw him suddenly go pale and lean against the wall to steady himself.

'Are you okay?' she asked him.

'Just cold. Although I inhabit this mammal body my mind is still reptilian. I need heat to function effectively.'

Tori led him to a radiator where he warmed his hands.

Mr Taylor did a headcount. All present and correct. He cleared his throat. 'Okay. Listen up, rabble.' He handed each of them a piece of paper covered in type so faded it looked like it had been photocopied at least two hundred times. 'You'll see there are twenty questions. Each answer relates to a different exhibit in the museum. I want you to fill in the answers as you go. It's a sort of quiz. Quite dull, but at least it's short.'

The children began to disperse, drifting away to the various halls that adjoined the entrance lobby. Tori turned to Admiral Skink, but saw that he had wandered off to look at the pile of rocks in the corner of the lobby. She caught up with him.

'What is this?' he said in a quiet voice, staring at the pile.

'It's a triceratops,' said Tori. 'A dinosaur.'

'It. . . is a reptile, is it not? Like me.'

'Yes.'

'Look at these horns. It is a warrior!'

'I suppose so,' said Tori. 'They lived on this planet millions of years ago. There were hundreds of different species. They were the dominant form of life.'

'*Were?*'

'They all died out.'

'Why? Was the planet invaded by your mammal race? Did you exterminate them all?' Admiral Skink said, feeling anger flaring up inside him.

Tori smiled. 'No, a big meteorite hit the Earth. It wiped out most forms of life, dinosaurs included. We mammals just filled the gap they left behind.'

169

Admiral Skink stared at the huge skull in wonder. He shook his head slowly. 'To see these creatures in their savage prime – that would be worth something.'

'The meteorite's on display in the Hall of Minerals,' said Tori softly. 'That's that one over there.' She pointed to a hallway close to the museum's main entrance. 'Are you ready?'

'Yes, let us not delay.'

Tori touched his arm. 'It's weird,' she said. 'Much as I miss Lance and want him back, I'm going to miss you too.' She smiled warmly and trotted towards another of the galleries.

'You are too kind,' called Admiral Skink, adding under his breath, 'and that is why you are so pathetically easy to deceive.'

Admiral Skink gazed at the lump of silvery-black metal before him. Under the hall's flickering yellow strip lights the meteorite shone with a hard, glassy brilliance. It was finally over, he thought.

He scanned the hall for something heavy that he could use to strike the meteorite. All the display cases he could see contained either tiny rocks or notes explaining that they should contain tiny rocks, but someone had unfortunately lost them during the last spring clean. He clicked his tongue in irritation. Then he noticed the security guard. He was a fat man in a dark uniform perched on a stool reading a newspaper near the entrance to the hall, paying no attention to the bored schoolchildren wandering in and out.

The stool, thought Admiral Skink. That would probably do the job. All that remained now was for. . .

'Wah!!! A lizard!!!'

Right on cue, the bizarre hysterical sound reverberated around the entire museum, followed by excited laughter and cheering. The few children mooching about in the Hall of Minerals looked at each other with widening eyes and then dashed off in the direction of the noise. More laughter followed – and the sound of breaking glass.

'Oh blimey,' said the security guard, putting down his paper. 'What the ruddy heck can that be?' He prised himself off his stool and waddled towards the commotion as fast as his stubby legs would carry him.

Admiral Skink watched him disappear

through the hallway. He was alone now in the Hall of Minerals. He picked up the security guard's stool and carried it towards the meteorite. He raised the stool high above his head.

'The Grand Ruler of the Swerdlixian Lizard Swarm will have his revenge,' he muttered through clenched teeth – and then slammed down the stool on to the meteorite with all the might he could muster. The meteorite shattered with the force of a small bomb, sending thousands of tiny metal fragments flying in all directions. Admiral Skink shielded his eyes, waiting until the echoes of the blow had died away. Then he peeped through a crack in his fingers.

There on the display stand, amid countless glassy shards of broken meteorite, lay a small

rectangle of shiny black metal inscribed with weird alien hieroglyphs. The memory wafer. His heart leaped.

'Thank the Great Lizard God Kyross,' he whispered and reached for it.

A pudgy hand got there before him. It snatched away the memory wafer.

'I'll have that, I reckon,' said the owner of the pudgy hand, Rick Thrattle. 'Oh, and by the way, you are gonna get in so much trouble for breaking this meteorite, Spratface. I'll see to that.'

Admiral Skink's jaw flopped open. 'Give me that!' he hissed, his whole body quaking with indignation. 'It is more important than you can possibly know.' He reached for the memory wafer, but Rick held it high above his head, teasing him.

174

'What's got into you and your little girlfriend today?' said Rick, shoving Admiral Skink painfully to the floor with one hand. 'Some mad lizard leaped out of her bag and started knocking over all the displays. Now you're smashing up meteorites and finding weird gizmos inside them. What is this? National Nerds Act Even Stupider Than Usual Day?'

'Give me what you are holding,' said Admiral Skink, rising to his feet and removing the ARGH from his inside pocket. He pointed it at Rick. 'Give it to me now. I mean it.'

Rick snorted. 'You're going to shoot me with your telly remote control? What are you going to do? Change my channel? Don't make me laugh, you loser. You're a typical nerd, aren't you? Don't know the first thing about

175

fighting. Too busy with your weedy science stuff. Your type really makes me–'

A stream of blue-white flames erupted from the end of the ARGH and streaked through the air towards Rick, missing his head by millimetres. The flames slammed into the wall behind him, vaporising several bricks with a dazzling flash of light.

Rick stared open-mouthed at the smoking hole in the wall. He spun on his heels and bolted out of the hall, still clutching the memory wafer.

'Come back, you thieving mammal!' roared Admiral Skink and set off after him. Pelting across the hall, he felt a wicked surge of

adrenaline in his belly. The ARGH had worked! And now there was havoc to be created!

Rick skidded into the entrance lobby, nearly colliding with a cabinet full of Edwardian horse brasses. Mr Taylor and Tori were coming into the entrance lobby. Tori was clutching her school bag to her chest and looking mortally embarrassed.

'I don't know how Pickles got in there,' she was saying. 'He's normally such a well-behaved lizard. Don't worry, I'll take him straight home at lunchtime.'

'Mr Taylor! Sir! Sir! Lancespratleyhasgot alasergunandhesblownupstuffandhesafter meand—'

'Rick?' Mr Taylor stared in surprise at the pale, breathless boy panting before him. 'Whatever's up with you, lad? Take

177

a minute to get your breath back.'

Rick leaned forward, hands on knees, his chest heaving. 'Sir,' he gasped, 'it's. . . Lance. . . He's got. . . a. . . laser gun. . .'

'A laser gun?' said Mr Taylor. 'Oh I see. You're playing one of your space games. *Zork Doodah – Slayer of Thingummies*, is it?'

'No. . . sir. . . It's. . . re–'

'Well I'm afraid,' said Mr Taylor, cutting him off, 'that your little game will have to end. You should be filling in your activity sheet. The museum is no place for fun, you know.'

Tori's eyes narrowed. 'A laser gun, you say? What did it look like?'

A section of wall behind Tori's head exploded in a shower of blue sparks.

ZZZZZSSSSSCCCHHHHHHHHHHHH
AAAAAAAAAAAAP!

'Pretty much like that,' said Rick.

'What the devil's going on?' said Mr Taylor.

Around them children screamed and dived for cover behind display cabinets. Thinking there might be a fire, the museum's staff tried hurriedly to decide which of the exhibits they ought to save. They soon reached the conclusion that it was all junk and scarpered via the nearest exit.

'I tried to tell you,' said Rick, waving his hands to dispel the choking smoke. 'But you wouldn't listen. . .' Suddenly he felt a hand snatch the memory wafer from his grasp. 'Hey!' he called. 'That's mine!'

A laugh echoed around the smoky hall, a long, booming, gleeful cackle. A laugh filled with unspeakable pleasure and unspeakable relief.

179

And unspeakable evil too.

Rick let out a high shriek and hid himself, quaking, behind Mr Taylor.

'Hello?' said Tori.

The smoke cleared, revealing the skinny figure of an eleven-year-old boy standing in the centre of the hall. In one hand he held a device a little like a television remote control. In the other he held a small dark rectangle of metal.

Mr Taylor stared at the figure in disbelief. 'Lance?' he said. 'Lance Spratley? What have you done here? What on earth is going on?'

'What is going on,' said Admiral Skink, surveying the three humans before him with regal disdain, 'is nothing to do with anything *on Earth*. That shall become plain very soon.'

'You've got it!' said Tori. 'Wowee! That's fantastic!'

Admiral Skink held aloft the memory wafer. He pressed one of the symbols set into it with his thumb. A yellow light began to wink steadily. 'The homing beacon is activated,' he said.

'That's brilliant,' said Tori. 'I'm so pleased you're finally able to go home. When will you be able to let Lance have his body back?'

'Oh, how about. . . *never?*' he said with a

smirk. 'When I am done with this feeble human form I shall have it ejected into space as the piece of refuse it undoubtedly is.'

'What?' screamed Tori. Her legs wobbled. She suddenly felt sick to her stomach. 'You wouldn't do that to my friend! You can't! We had an agreement!'

'Ah yes, the agreement. . .' said Admiral Skink. 'Unfortunately, I am actually really rather, well, *evil,* when it comes down to it and I have no intention whatsoever of honouring our little pact. So, sorry. But that's evil for you, I'm afraid.'

Hot tears began to form in the corner of Tori's eyes. She bit her lip and balled her fists.

Admiral Skink swung the ARGH to aim at Rick and Mr Taylor. 'You two,' he hissed.

182

'Us?' said Rick and Mr Taylor in unison, quivering.

'You have both caused me much pain and humiliation since my arrival on this dung heap of a world. Had I the time and resources I would punish you as we punish all wrongdoers on my world – by smearing them in warm marmalade and dropping them into a pit of Iggleflimpian Razor Termites. But do not fear.' He grinned. 'Your deaths will still be excruciatingly painful.'

His thumb slid across the top of the ARGH to its trigger button. He pressed down on it.

Nothing happened.

'Idiotic thing's jammed!' hissed Admiral Skink. He held the device to his ear and rattled it.

With a joint shriek of terror, Rick and Mr Taylor suddenly sprinted off across the hall, their feet pounding against the wooden floor. Admiral Skink grunted in annoyance. He aimed the ARGH at the two fleeing forms and jabbed the button again. This time it worked and a stream of glittering fire shot out.

The sparks and smoke began once more to clear, revealing Rick and Mr Taylor cowering in a corner next to the triceratops skull.

'Look!' shouted Tori. 'The dinosaur!'

'Can you all please keep quiet for one moment?' said Admiral Skink. 'You'll all be disintegrated soon enough. There's no rush.'

Then something caught his eye. A weird, bluish glow. There was a bright halo of light

184

encircling the triceratops skull. Rick backed away from it, whimpering.

Interesting, thought Admiral Skink. The ARGH was designed to vaporise non-living matter and to turn living matter into sludgy blue goo – but he had no idea what would happen when its beam encountered the *fossilised* remains of living matter. He watched as the blue aura steadily engulfed the huge stone skull. There was a heavy throbbing noise and sparks flew from its surface. The skull... *juddered;* Admiral Skink was sure of it. Its great jaws appeared briefly to open and close, as if snapping at a fly. Was this some optical illusion? Perhaps the skull had absorbed so much energy it was about to explode? It *juddered* again, the great horned head shaking slowly from

side to side as if waking from a monumental slumber. Blue light coalesced behind the skull. Flames congealed and hardened into tough sinewy flesh and iron-hard plates of bone. The missing horn regrew with a crackle of blue sparks. Admiral Skink watched, trembling with wonder, as the great armoured face opened wide its huge curved beak and emitted a roar of pure reptilian fury unheard on the planet for sixty-five million years.

CHAPTER TEN
THE PATIENCE OF LIZARDS

The blackness of space was ablaze with brilliant pinpricks of light.

The pinpricks of light were the starships of the Swerdlixian lizard Swarm joyfully blowing one another to bits.

Swerdlixian Lizards are not noted for their patience. Indeed, if you asked a Swerdlixian lizard to rate his patience on a scale of one

to ten, he would kill you, explaining as his huge scaly claw squeezed the trigger of his disintegrator pistol, that he had no time to waste on stupid questions about patience. That's how little patience they have.

The principal interests of Swerdlixian lizards are, as you have probably gathered by now, war, destruction, pushing around inferior forms of life, more war, more destruction, blowing things up, a bit more war, pulverising things and being generally awful in as many other ways as possible.

Consequently, when the Swerdlixian Lizard Swarm found themselves unexpectedly without their leader, it wasn't long before they tired of waiting for Admiral Skink to return and started attacking one

another for no other reason than it seemed like a fun way to spend the afternoon.

Captain Gila's starship careered through interstellar space, guns blazing wildly at any vessel within sensor range. He had already blown up over a dozen ships from his own fleet. He sniggered to himself, wiping a trickle of drool off his stubby green snout. How proud their leader would be when he returned to his troops! Admiral Skink would see that they had used their time wisely. A Swerdlixian lizard revelled in destruction, even if it was pointless.

Especially if it was pointless.

A blip of yellow light appeared on Captain Gila's vision screen. From its outline he identified it as a ship called *The Krockatrix* –

a vessel piloted by a particularly fearsome lizard called Commodore Tuatara.

Captain Gila's lips curled into a hideous reptilian parody of a smile. At military academy, Tuatara used to steal Gila's dinner money, and had once pushed Gila's head into a bowl of Scramthorn stew.

Payback time!

Captain Gila's fat clawed finger slid to the trigger button of his ship's laser cannon. On a whim, he flipped a switch opening a communication channel to *The Krockatrix*.

'Commodore Tuatara!' he roared. 'You made my younger years a misery. To this day I cannot look at a Scramthorn plant without being reminded of the sickening humiliation you put me through. Prepare to die!'

Commodore Tuatara's defiant voice

snapped back over the communicator. 'I do not fear you, Captain Gila! You are a worthless coward with the intelligence of a Pentaxian Slop Beetle! Make no mistake about it; it is *you* who shall die!'

'Cobblers!' shouted Captain Gila and stabbed at the firing button of his laser cannon.

It failed to fire.

'Whuh?' he stammered. He checked his sensor readout. A sudden unexplained loss of weapon power. . .

191

'What's going on?' called Commodore Tuatara. 'All my weapons are jammed.'

'Mine too,' replied Captain Gila. 'I don't know what's causing–'

A shrill electronic voice interrupted him.

'Emergency! Emergency! This is an automatic message. All weapons systems have been temporarily disabled to ensure your attention. Admiral Skink, the Glorious Leader of the Swerdlixian Lizard Swarm, is trapped on a nearby planet and awaiting rescue. A guiding signal is being transmitted to the navigation computers of all Swerdlixian starships within range. In short, stop scrapping with one another and go and pick him up! The Admiral has used Mind Migration technology to disguise himself. Full details of his current appearance

and location are being transmitted to your vision screens now. Thank you for choosing Braintwizzler™, the name to trust in modern immortality solutions.'

Captain Gila's cold lizard heart raced.

'Did you hear that?' asked Commodore Tuatara. 'Our Admiral needs us.'

'I did,' said Captain Gila. 'It is time to set aside our petty grievances and unite once more as loyal troops of the Swerdlixian Lizard Swarm.'

'Agreed.'

In the airless wastes of space, the million pinpricks that were the starships of the Swerdlixian Lizard Swarm ceased their battle and came together in formation. They set off as one, engines roaring, guided automatically towards their goal by the

emergency signal beaming through space from Admiral Skink's memory wafer.

Two images appeared on Captain's Gila's vision screen. One was of a hideous ape-like creature, identified by a caption with the bizarrely alien name Lance Spratley. Captain Gila snorted in disgust. The other image showed a pleasant blue-white planet. It was labelled Earth. Beneath the label was some text. It read:

ONCE RESCUE IS MISSION CARRIED OUT, ALL LIFE ON THIS PLANET IS TO BE ANNIHILATED.

CHAPTER ELEVEN
LOTS OF THINGS GET SMASHED

The triceratops shook itself. Its massive tail rippled, shattering two display cases filled with Georgian-era cutlery and upending a rack of faded postcards. It stared at Admiral Skink with two small curious eyes set deep within its enormous horned face.

Tori's mouth formed a silent 'wowee'. She reached for Mr Taylor's hand but he wasn't there. She turned and saw him and Rick disappear through the hole in the wall like frightened rabbits. She dived behind an overturned bench and peeped over.

Admiral Skink placed his hand gently against the bony frill surrounding the triceratops's skull. 'Fellow lizard,' he whispered. 'Feel my mind reaching out to yours. Feel it expanding your own mind. Feel your awareness increasing, your intelligence multiplying. No longer are you a lowly creature. You are an honoured member of my household! To whom do you owe your newfound intellect? To whom do you owe your lifelong loyalty?'

The beast opened its huge bony beak. 'To Admiral Skink!' it boomed, in a rumbling voice as ancient as rock that echoed around

the ruined entrance lobby. Admiral Skink clambered onto the creature's back and gripped the bony frill surrounding its head.

He rubbed his hands together. 'Time for a spot of wanton destruction and planet-conquering, I think. Walk on!'

The triceratops lumbered forward, its elephantine feet trampling over the museum's wrecked exhibits. With a flick of its mighty horned head, it smashed through the main door and waddled out onto the street.

'You again is it, Mo?'

Police Constable Geoffrey Sledge heaved a sigh. It was the sheer lack of challenge that annoyed him. As a thief, Mo had little technique or finesse; she belonged to the

grab-it-and-scarper school of shoplifting. He was pretty sure he hadn't joined the force to arrest the same mad old woman for nicking Hobnobs five times a week.

He stared out of the shop window, lost momentarily in his wistful longing, at the crushing ordinariness of a Monday morning in Cottleton town centre: the cars at the traffic lights belching their white fumes into the cold air; the dull shopfronts with their untempting bargains; the shoppers in their overcoats and scarves hurrying along; the huge dinosaur rampaging along the High Street with a laughing boy perched on its back, smashing everything in its path. . .

He shook himself, rubbed his eyes, then ran to the door, pressing his face hard against the glass. A girl with a mop of curly hair ran

up to the window. Wasn't she one of the kids he'd met tramping about in the forest the other night? Through the glass she mouthed the words *We need to talk* at him.

'Oi!' called the shopkeeper, gesturing at the elderly woman with five packets of biscuits protruding from under her large woolly hat. 'What's more important than dealing with this old villain?'

In a voice filled with wonder PC Sledge turned and whispered the word *'Pizzazz'* before running out of the shop and into the most extraordinary day of his entire life.

STOMP. STOMP. STOMP. STOMP. SMASH!

Three iron-hard horns crashed through the window of a cut-price fashion store, each one spearing a tailor's dummy through the

199

chest. The horns held aloft the mannequins' impaled bodies in a show of victory and then flung them away. A rain of plastic body parts thudded onto the pavement.

For the first time since arriving on Earth, Admiral Skink felt truly at peace. As the triceratops trotted along the High Street, flattening everything it encountered, sending people scurrying in all directions and dropping their shopping, he felt a broad cheek-aching grin take control of his face. There was something pure about destruction, something simple and true about the causing of needless misery to others. It was a feeling he had gone without for too long and his heart sang with cold-blooded lizard pleasure to have it back.

He gave the triceratops's bony neck frill a sharp twist like a steering wheel and the great beast turned and began to lumber in a new direction.

With a satisfying *thump!* Mr Spratley slammed the final nail into place. He stood back, nodding approvingly, and replaced the hammer in his toolbox. 'You've got to admit,' he said to Mrs Spratley and Sally, who were standing beside him, 'that this is a fine bit of handiwork.' He sucked at a wood splinter in his thumb.

In the background a radio burbled quietly to itself: '. . .creature still at large. Citizens are advised to stay in their homes and lock all windows and doors. . .'

Neither his wife nor his daughter spoke.

They stared at the rough wooden planks covering the living room window. Between the planks only the tiniest slivers of daylight shone into the living room, casting it into a glum semi-darkness.

'Solid, that is,' he said. 'I'd like to see any dinosaur get through that little lot. I knew that wood would come in handy. To think I was going to build a shed with it. Glad I didn't now. What's more important than protecting your family, eh?'

Mrs Spratley reached out and prodded at the wooden defence with her finger. She expected it to wobble, but was surprised when it held firm. 'Not bad – I suppose,' she said. She always found praising her husband difficult. She'd had so little practice. 'You reckon that's going

203

to keep out this dinosaur thingy, then?'

'No doubt about it,' said Mr Spratley. He rapped the wood with his knuckle. 'Listen to that. Best quality pine.'

'I have to say,' said Mrs Spratley with a small smile, 'that I'm pleasantly surprised by the quality of the job. I didn't think you had it in you. Not after the incident with the bookshelf above Sally's bed. Poor girl still gets headaches. But this is a nice bit of DIY. Well done.' She patted his arm.

Mr Spratley's cheeks reddened in the half-light. 'Thank you, dear,' he said. 'That means a lot. In times of danger, a man is called upon to protect his home and family and he must answer that call. It is an age-old duty and I am glad you feel I have fulfilled it to the best of my—'

'Where's Lance?' said Sally suddenly. After news of the rogue dinosaur spread, the schools had closed early as parents insisted on collecting their children and bringing them home. In all the excitement, Sally had quite forgotten about her brother. She was not, it appeared, the only one.

'Um, who?' said Mr Spratley.

'Lance!' cried Mrs Spratley. 'Where is he? Where's our son?'

Mr Spratley booted the skirting board in frustration. 'Blast it! I knew I'd forgotten something. Where's he got to?'

'Oh, I can imagine,' said Mrs Spratley. 'He's probably standing at the school gate wondering why we haven't come to pick him up in the car. Lazy little tyke! The walk home wouldn't kill him. This is *so* typical!

You spend hours safeguarding our home from ravening monsters and that idle good-for-nothing can't even be bothered to be here to be protected.'

Mr Spratley said nothing. He knew it was better not to interrupt his wife when she was in full flow like this.

'Just you wait 'til I see him,' Mrs Spratley went on. 'I'll have a few words to say to that young man. Oh, yes. Why does he always have to spoil everything for the rest of us?'

A hand rapped hard on the shop door. 'Open up! Hand over all your ice lollies and ice creams!' called a voice.

Silence.

Another rap on the door – loud, insistent. 'Come on! We need those ice lollies!

Time is very much of the essence here!'

Mr Holland, the grocer, peered over his shop counter. 'Go away!' he shouted. 'There'll be no looting here. Dinosaur or no dinosaur, we shall behave like civilised human beings and respect the rule of law. I have a cricket bat, you know, and I'm prepared to use it to defend my property. So unless you want a smart crack on the noggin, I suggest you be on your way.'

'This is the police,' said the voice. 'We're on official business. We urgently need all your stocks of ice lollies and ice creams and we need them right now. If you don't open this door, we shall have to break it in. I'm sorry but you leave us no option.'

'Whoa, whoa, whoa,' said Mr Holland, springing up from behind the counter.

'Let's not be so hasty.' He unlocked the door. Outside were a police officer and a young schoolgirl with a mop of unkempt fair hair. Both were carrying large, brightly coloured plastic bazookas. Mr Holland eyed the weapons uneasily. 'What is this?' he said. *'Buck Rogers in the 25th Century?'*

'This,' said Constable Sledge, striking a pose with his gun, 'is the Mega-Douser 500, the most powerful water pistol ever invented.'

'We got them from the toyshop next door,' explained Tori. 'The shopkeeper was ever so helpful.'

'So hand over all your ice lollies,' said Sledge. 'Pronto.'

Mr Holland blinked at them in confusion.

'We don't mean to sound bossy,' said Tori.

'It's just that we're in a bit of a hurry to save the world.'

With tank-like relentlessness, the triceratops waddled along the street towards the Spratley residence, flattening two tricycles and a vintage sports car in its path. On Admiral Skink's face an expression of deep and vicious contentment began to spread like a dark stain. A shiver of anticipation passed through his body, the pre-battle thrill of bloodlust familiar to all warriors throughout history. This was going to be a right old laugh.

The triceratops advanced along the Spratleys' garden path, its elephantine feet leaving great round indentations in the grey tarmac. Standing in front of the house was

a collection of old furniture and household appliances including a chipped sideboard and a yellowing fridge. They were piled up, creating a rough barrier.

'Look, the monkeys have built themselves a barricade,' snorted Admiral Skink, releasing a wisp of white vapour from his nose into the cold air. 'Let's show them what we think of barricades.'

The triceratops jabbed its head forward, shattering the barricade and spearing the fridge's door on one of its horns. The beast shook its head and flung the door high into the air. It clattered onto the path.

From within the house came a shriek of terror.

'Oh, good,' said Admiral Skink. 'They're in.'

Four eyes and two noses appeared over a nearby hedge. The eyes watched as Admiral Skink clambered down from the triceratops and approached the Spratleys' house, its four front windows rendered blank and imposing by the wooden planks nailed across them. Admiral Skink pressed lightly against the front door, testing its strength. It swung open, not even locked. He guffawed and went in.

'Why's he gone into that house?' said PC Sledge.

'Old scores to settle,' said Tori. She cocked her water pistol. 'Time to move in.'

They padded along the garden path, keeping low.

'You stay outside by the door,' whispered Tori. 'I'll go in and try to reason with him.'

211

She turned and gasped, her path blocked by a strange grey-green wall that had appeared from nowhere. She stepped back, bewildered, her heart hammering.

It was the triceratops.

'Leave, little creatures,' it boomed in its rumbling avalanche of a voice. 'The Admiral has business inside and he is not to be disturbed. Go – or face the consequences.'

PC Sledge raised his water pistol. Tori shook her head and he lowered it again. She took a step towards the immense creature, her hands outstretched in a gesture of friendliness. 'You realise what Admiral Skink is going to do, don't you?' she said to it.

'He is going to conquer this planet,' said the triceratops. 'And it is my honour to assist.'

'That's right,' said Tori. 'And I think that's extremely generous of you when you consider that this is *your* planet he's conquering.'

The triceratops blinked its two tiny eyes at her. 'Come again?'

'This is your planet,' said Tori. 'You dinosaurs ruled it for millions of years. You went away of course, but now you're back. This world is your inheritance – and now you're handing it over to an alien. Very generous, as I said.

Giving away so freely what is rightfully yours.'
She smiled pleasantly.

The triceratops cocked its enormous head
to one side like a bird. 'Explain that to me
one more time,' it said.

'Lance Spratley – where on *earth* do you think
you've been?'

Admiral Skink smiled as he sauntered into
the living room. He yawned and sat down on
the sofa.

'Don't you know there's a dinosaur out
there?' Mrs Spratley continued. 'Couldn't
you hear it? Why didn't you come home
straight from school?'

Admiral Skink snorted. 'I have been trying
to get *home* for some considerable time.
But no matter. Come. Let me look at you,

you Spratleys. I want to remember you just the way you are.'

'What are you on about?' said Mrs Spratley. A thought occurred. She turned to her husband. 'How did he get in? I thought you said we were safe? If an eleven-year-old boy can slip through your defences what chance do we stand against dinosaurs?'

Mr Spratley clapped a hand to his forehead. 'The front door!' he hissed. 'I'll get my toolbox.'

'No, stay,' said Admiral Skink. 'I want to tell you all something.'

'What? What is it, lad?' said Mr Spratley.

Admiral Skink laughed. He looked from Mr Spratley to Mrs Spratley and then to Sally, who was sitting on a footstool pretending to scratch her nose but actually

215

picking it. 'I want to tell you that you inhabitants of the planet Earth are without doubt the foulest and most wretched creatures I have ever encountered in all my years of space travel – and it will now be my extreme personal pleasure to deprive you of your stupid, stupid lives. Prepare for death.' He took out the ARGH.

'Is that the telly remote?' said Mr Spratley, frowning.

Mrs Spratley rolled her eyes. 'This isn't the time for your stupid imagination, Lance.'

'And now,' said Admiral Skink, 'I'm afraid that something extremely unpleasant indeed is going to happen to you. Goodbye.' He pointed the ARGH at them.

Suddenly, there came a sound like colliding oil tankers, or possibly like a brass band

falling down an escalator. In fact it was the sound of a fully-grown triceratops smashing its way through the Spratleys' living room window, shattering the wooden planks nailed across them as easily as lolly sticks, and landing on the hearthrug.

The Spratleys howled in shock and terror.

'How dare you interrupt me at my moment of revenge!' cried Admiral Skink. 'Bad dinosaur! Out! Out of here!' He made shooing motions.

'This is my planet!' rumbled the triceratops. It swung its great bony face towards Admiral Skink, its nose-horn mere centimetres from his chest. 'You shall not take it from me.'

'You brainless lump!' spat Admiral Skink. 'Do you think the Grand Ruler of the Swerdlixian Lizard Swarm is going to be

stopped by an overgrown newt like you? I brought you to life and I can send you back to extinction just as easily.' He raised the ARGH.

But before he could activate the weapon, something struck him in the chest. Something cold and wet. Admiral Skink staggered backwards. A black wave of nausea passed over him. Then another attack came, this time from another angle, striking him on the shoulder. He looked down, his vision dimming. He was covered in brightly coloured goo. It was freezing to the touch. Painful tingles paralysed his fingers and toes.

Dimly, Admiral Skink became aware of two humanoid figures clambering into the room through the wrecked window.

'Neapolitan,' said one of the figures.

'What?' said Admiral Skink faintly. His teeth were chattering. He squinted upwards and then recognised her. 'Ah,' he said. 'You.'

Tori trained the bulbous plastic gun directly at him. 'Delicious Neapolitan ice cream,' she said. 'Just the thing to slow down a cold-blooded lizard. What you are experiencing now is brain-freeze of an extraordinary magnitude.' She motioned at the other figure. 'This is Constable Sledge. His ammunition of choice is ground-up ice lolly. Mint flavour. Now, drop the weapon, there's a good space lizard.'

Admiral Skink sighed. 'A good warrior admits when he is beaten,' he said. Then a sly look appeared on his face. He clicked his fingers.

219

Pickles the iguana exploded out of Tori's shoulder bag. Tori dropped her water pistol in surprise. With lightning speed Pickles sprang at PC Sledge and nipped his fingers with his tiny spiky teeth. PC Sledge yelped and let go of his weapon.

Admiral Skink kicked the two water pistols out of their reach. He backed into the corner of the room, the ARGH raised, his eyes wide with evil delight.

'And this warrior is not beaten yet!'

CHAPTER TWELVE
SMART—ALEC MAMMAL

The black door opened and then slammed shut with a clang.

'Hello,' said Lance.

The receptionist looked up from her work.

'Having a nice day?' said Lance. 'I am.' He gave her a cheery wink.

'You're very chipper for someone who's just had a session with the Fear, Pain and Misery

Specialists,' said the receptionist. 'You don't look like the type who could withstand their treatment. I had you down as the sort who would cave in and beg for mercy instantly.' She gave a smirk.

There was a sudden flash of white light. A metal cage started to form around the receptionist. Her greeny-yellow eyes opened wide in surprise.

'This is an inescapable cage,' said Lance. 'Once inside you will not be able to get out without causing a logical contradiction and the computer creating this virtual world won't allow that.'

With a loud popping noise the receptionist turned herself into a long blue snake and slithered smartly out of the cage before it had finished creating itself around her.

'But what if I was never fully in the cage to begin with? Then I do not have to escape, do I?' she hissed. There was a *pop* and she became her usual self again. 'What do you think of that, you smart-alec mammal? You may understand the rules of this computer-generated environment but that doesn't make you unbeatable.'

Lance froze, flummoxed. He had not expected that.

The receptionist transformed herself into a huge three-headed crocodile with long gleaming teeth. 'You're not dealing with those two fools Sludgeclaw and Whiptail now,' she hissed savagely. 'I can imagine even more horrible things than them! I used to be a Fear, Pain and Misery Specialist myself but the management

reckoned I was too vicious so they made me a receptionist instead.'

The crocodile reared over Lance, its awful growls and snarls mingling with the monotonous background music.

Lance cowered, gibbering. He tried to think of some shape he could assume to defeat the crocodile but his mind was suddenly blank. Not a single idea came to him. He felt himself slide to the floor, his limbs melting with terror.

'Oh, blimey,' he muttered, screwing his eyes shut. 'I wish you could be a bit more helpful. I really do.'

There was a popping sound.

The receptionist reverted to her usual form, only now she was smiling pleasantly. 'It would be my pleasure to assist you in any way I can, sir,' she said.

'What?' said Lance, his eyes narrowing. 'Weren't you just going to eat me?'

'I was.'

'But you're not now?'

'No. Unless you want me to transform back into a three-headed crocodile? Would you like that?'

'No!' said Lance suddenly. 'I wouldn't.'

'As you wish, sir. Happy to help in any way.'

Lance frowned – and then clicked his fingers. 'That's it! I wished you could be a bit more helpful and the computer's turned you into a helpful version of yourself!'

'Correct, sir,' said the receptionist. 'You appear to have reprogrammed my personality at a fundamental level. I exist now simply to aid you in your wishes. What is it I may do for you?'

'I need to get my body back,' said Lance. 'Any suggestions?'

'Not as simple as it sounds, unfortunately,' said the receptionist. 'Although we can

control the memory wafer from this computer, we can't simply snatch Admiral Skink's mind out of your body without his permission, which he's not likely to give until he's safely back on Swerdlix. His mind is embedded very deeply in the structure of your brain now. It would take a huge emotional shock – some kind of terrible fright, say – to make his mind loosen its hold enough so that the memory wafer could reabsorb it.'

'A terrible fright, eh?' Lance pointed a finger at the receptionist's computer. 'It says **MEMORY STATION** – are these Admiral Skink's memories in here?'

'Correct, sir.'

'Let me see.'

The receptionist clicked the file icon on

the screen and it opened, revealing a patchwork of images. 'This is Admiral Skink's life,' she said. 'I've been cataloguing his memories. Right from when he was an egg. It's all here. Cheating on his military academy exams, blackmailing his way to the top, wiping out endangered alien species. . .'

'Great. So, this memory wafer we're on,' said Lance. 'It stores images and information, right?'

'That's correct, sir,' said the receptionist sweetly.

'How easy would it be to make it project images and information out into the real world?'

'No trouble at all, sir. A simple matter of reversing a certain polarity. I suspect sir has some plan of his own up his sleeve.

Am I correct?'

'Maybe,' replied Lance, thoughtfully. 'Can we find out where the wafer is right now?'

'Certainly,' said the receptionist. 'The device is equipped with an external scanner.' She clicked a button on the screen. An image appeared.

Lance's eyes nearly popped out of his head.

CHAPTER THIRTEEN
'WHAT'S MORE TERRIFYING THAN AN ALIEN LIZARD WARLORD?'

Pickles hopped over to Admiral Skink and stood next to him like an obedient pet. He stuck out his tiny pink tongue at the others.

'So,' said Admiral Skink, 'I do believe I was in the process of disintegrating a lot of stupid mammals.' He eyed the triceratops, which was looking somewhat dazed by events. 'And one stupid traitorous reptile too.

Prepare to die, blah blah blah. No need to say it all again.' He raised the ARGH.

There was a popping sound. Admiral Skink paused and looked up. Then what colour he had drained completely from his face.

A glowing shape was forming in front of him. It was the image of a female lizard of his own species, a wizened old creature with bulbous bloodshot eyes and saggy wrinkled skin. She threw back her head and roared fiercely, emitting a blazing torrent of fire from her mouth.

Admiral Skink screamed and dropped the ARGH. 'Mother?' he whimpered 'Is that you? How did you get here?'

'SKINK!' bellowed the old lizard. 'Haven't you conquered this pathetic little world yet? Too busy messing about and daydreaming

if I know you. Typical! So very typical! You were always such a crushing disappointment to me.'

'I – I – I'm sorry,' he stammered in a small voice. 'I'm trying my best. Honestly!'

'Oh, do shut up, there's a good boy,' said the old lizard. 'I get so tired of your constant snivelling.'

'Mother!' hissed Admiral Skink. 'You're embarrassing me in front of the Earth creatures!'

'I don't want to hear any more,' said the old lizard, waving a stern claw at him. 'I think it's time you had a little rest. You're obviously overtired and showing off. I shan't put up with such behaviour. Time for bed, young Skinky.'

'No, Mother! I'm fine! I'm not tired–'

But before Admiral Skink could say another word there was a popping sound and a flash of white light. The old lizard creature vanished. Admiral Skink staggered backwards, falling onto the Spratleys' sofa. A moment passed.

'Lance!' cried Mrs Spratley, snapping out of a sudden daze. 'What was all that about?'

The boy blinked and opened his eyes. 'Oh, hello,' he said, a little uncertainly. He looked around the room and at the faces of the people in it as if he was seeing them for the first time in ages, which, of course, he was. He waved at his friend. 'Hey, Tori. How's it going? There seems to be a triceratops in my living room. Cool!'

Tori gasped. 'Lance? Is that you?'

The boy nodded.

'Wowee! You're back! What happened?'

Lance grinned. 'I looked into his memories, found out his worst fear and confronted him with it. What's more terrifying than an alien lizard warlord? An alien lizard warlord's mum.' He giggled and took the memory wafer from his top pocket. He pressed a small symbol set into it. The yellow light stopped flashing.

'What have you done?'

'Turned off the homing signal,' said Lance. That'll throw his friends off the scent.'

'So what's happened to Admiral Skink?'

'His mind's trapped in this gizmo now.' He showed Tori the memory wafer. 'But if I can escape from it then it shouldn't take him long to figure it out too. But luckily I now know how to operate this technology. What we need to do is find another living organism

235

and transfer Admiral Skink's mind into it for good.'

'But where are we going to find a creature willing to do that?' said Tori.

'Here,' boomed the triceratops.

'It's very kind of you to volunteer,' said Tori. 'But just think how powerful Admiral Skink would be if he inhabited your body. He'd be unstoppable!'

'Not me,' said the triceratops. 'I mean this little sneak I just caught.' It gestured with its horned face to the squirming form of Pickles the iguana. He had obviously been trying to slope away but the triceratops had pinned him to the floor by his tail under one of its elephantine feet.

'But what will we do with him then?' said Tori.

'Leave it to me,' said PC Sledge. 'I'm sure we can find him some suitable accommodation.'

Mr and Mrs Spratley exchanged astonished looks, finding it difficult to understand anything that had happened in the last five minutes. Unable to think of anything else to do, Mrs Spratley thumped her husband. At least that made her feel normal.

Tori collapsed onto the sofa beside Lance. She gave him a hug and heaved a huge relieved sigh.

'Let's put the telly on!' cried Sally cheerfully. 'It's time for cartoons!' She picked up the ARGH.

'No!' cried Tori. 'That's the—'

But before she could finish speaking there was a blinding flash of blue light. When the after-images finally stopped dancing

before her eyes, she saw that Lance's sister, mother and father were no longer in the room. In their places were three wobbling heaps of blue jelly.

The engines of Captain Gila's starship suddenly went quiet. He felt the craft slow to a halt and begin to drift aimlessly.

'What in the name of Kyross the Lizard God. . .?'

The radio crackled. 'Captain Gila! Commodore Tuatara here. The guiding signal's gone dead! We've lost our path to the Admiral!'

'What?' snapped Captain Gila and checked his vision screen. It was true. The automatic signal had ceased as abruptly as it had started. There was

now no way of tracking down Admiral Skink –
which meant the Swerdlixian Lizard Swarm
was once more without a leader. He gave a
chuckle. 'In that case, Commodore, I believe
you and I have a little unfinished business
to attend to.' For a second time, Captain
Gila's fat clawed finger edged towards the
firing button of his laser cannon. . .

A huge explosion rocked Captain Gila's
starship.

'What???' he spluttered as instrument
panels exploded all around him, showering
him with sparks. 'What's going on?'

'Remember me?' said a low, rasping voice
from the radio.

'Er. . . no,' said Captain Gila. 'Should I?'

'Pah!' spat the voice. 'My name is Lieutenant
Gecko. We had a fight once during a picnic

239

at military academy. You made me lose three scales from my tail. Well now revenge shall be mine!'

'Ah yes,' said Captain Gila. 'I remember n–'

There was a very loud bang.

CHAPTER FOURTEEN
A FINGERNAIL, AN EYELASH AND A NASAL HAIR

'Are you sure this is going to work?' said Tori two hours later as she followed Lance into the utility room.

'Sure?' said Lance as he unplugged the keyboard from the computer. 'I've just spent the past couple of days trapped in a virtual world created by lizard creatures. How can I ever be sure of anything again?'

He sniggered and coiled up the keyboard's lead.

In the living room, Lance laid the keyboard on the coffee table. Using a magnifying glass and tweezers, he removed three tiny scraps of matter from between its keys. 'It's a good job I didn't clean this out after all,' he told her. With the tweezers he placed one scrap of matter on each of the three seats of the family sofa. 'There,' he said, picking up the ARGH.

'Talk me through this one more time,' said Tori.

'Okay,' said Lance. 'As far as I can work out, this is an atomic cellular reconfigurator. It turns organic matter to blue jelly and brings fossilised organic matter to life.'

'Right? I'm guessing I'm supposed to say

"right" to that. So what?'

'So, if we fire it at a piece of dead organic matter, it should reconstitute the original creature, just the way it did with the dinosaur, right?'

'Right.'

'So, taking one of Mum's horrible varnished fingernails, one of Sally's eyelashes and one of Dad's nasal hairs from the muck clogging up the keyboard. . .'

'Yuck! I can't believe those things were in there and I can't believe you can identify them so easily either!'

'Trust me,' said Lance. 'When you share a house with people as annoying as my family you grow to know every tiny thing about everyone. I could pick out one of Sally's eyelashes from of a line-up of a hundred.

243

I always find them stuck to the eyepieces of my binoculars after she's been using it to watch the telly in the living room from the kitchen.'

Tori laughed. 'I won't ask how you can identify your dad's nose hair, then.' She was strangely touched that Lance was so keen to reconstitute his family when they clearly drove him crazy.

Lance aimed the ARGH at the sofa. 'Just a tiny bit of power remaining,' he said. 'We only get one go at this.' He winked at her and then pressed the button.

Blue light streamed from the handset. There was a tremendous burst of crackling blue sparks. Lance cried out in pain, dropping the ARGH as it grew red-hot in his hand. The sparks vanished and the Spratley

244

living room was once again in silence.

'You all right, son? You look a bit dazed.' Lance felt a friendly hand on his shoulder. He opened his eyes and saw his dad smiling down at him. He was beaming a bright, pleasant smile.

'Probably a bit hungry,' said his mum with a wink. 'I know what'll fix that. Some freshly-made pancakes! I take it your friend's staying for tea, too?' Without waiting for an answer, she set off for the kitchen, humming a little tune to herself.

'Yay! Pancakes!' said Sally. 'You're the best brother in the world, Lance!' She hugged him and scampered from the room to wash her hands for tea.

'Look at the state of this place,' said Mr Spratley, eyeing the broken window and

245

rough pine planks nailed to the frame. 'Looks like a bomb's hit it. Better call in the professionals. Best to do these things properly. I'll go and look up some builders' details on the Internet.' He was about to leave when he noticed the keyboard on the coffee table. 'I'll be needing this, then,' he said and picked it up, adding, 'Blimey! This has seen better days, hasn't it? Better order a new one while I'm at it.' He got to the door and then noticed the three piles of wobbling blue jelly on the carpet. 'Don't worry about that,' he called to Lance. 'I'll get rid of that rubbish later.' He went out.

Lance raised his eyebrows at Tori. 'I'm not sure what went wrong, there,' he said. 'But that doesn't sound like my family. Maybe I misadjusted some setting. Perhaps

there's a tiny bit more power in this thing. . . '
He picked up the ARGH and began to fiddle with it.

Tori snatched the ARGH from him and held it behind her back.

'Hey!' said Lance.

'I'll tell you exactly what went wrong,' said Tori. 'Nothing.' And she laughed.

After a second, Lance began to laugh too.

EPILOGUE

In the bowels of Cottleton police station is a small little-used storage room. At the back of this room, near the radiator where it is warm, is a large glass tank somewhat like an aquarium, although it is more properly called a vivarium. It is unlike most vivariums (or 'viviaria' if you prefer) in that its glass walls are super-toughened. Inside are some twigs, two ultraviolet lamps, a layer of coarse gravel coating the floor, a thermometer, a water bottle and feeding tube, a large quantity of dandelion leaves and the body of a common iguana with the mind of an alien lizard warlord from beyond the stars trapped in it. This iguana skulks in a corner

of his vivarium, munching mouthfuls of what he refers to in his scratchy, piping voice as 'Scramthorn plants' and occasionally requesting he be brought something he called 'Dysonian sparkworms'. But no one knows where to get them.

The iguana is watched over and cared for daily by a police officer who is one of only three people in the world who know the iguana's astonishing true identity. The other two people are a pair of schoolchildren known as the Knowledge Warriors. Or Knowledge Champions. It depends which one you ask.

The cost of the lizard's care is met by a grant from Cottleton Museum, an organisation that has recently become phenomenally wealthy. It gives out lots of

grants these days, especially to people and institutions in Cottleton who might have had property damaged by recent events.

Whereas most museums strive to bring the past to life, Cottleton Museum actually has a live triceratops cantering about in a specially made paddock created for it in the rear car park, and regularly raises millions of pounds in sponsorship from companies who want to be associated with what is widely regarded as the most astonishing museum exhibit of any kind ever displayed. Thousands of people queue up to see it every day and view the 3-D IMAX film in the museum's new luxury cinema that recreates using startling computer graphics the day the triceratops ran amok in Cottleton's town centre. The triceratops

did once consider trying to take back its planet from the hordes of apes that have infested it, but on reflection decided it preferred the easy life, and actually quite enjoyed giving rides to schoolchildren.

No one knows where the triceratops came from or the identity of the young boy reportedly controlling it during its rampage. A boy called Rick Thrattle maintains it was someone from his class at school, but no one believes him. Most people in Cottleton wouldn't believe Rick Thrattle if he told them the sky was blue.

Despite the lack of publicity, the police officer is very proud of his unusual prisoner. He feels he gives the place a little pizzazz.

TO BE CONTINUED. . .